SHOOTING WAR!

There was a ritual to such a showdown. Sam shot Magrew with his left hand and Jackson with his right. They never had a chance to draw. Immediately he dropped to his knee and managed a lateral move. Stubby was doing the same.

Duffy seemed transfixed, his mouth open. Sam had to attend to the rifleman who, somewhat stupified by the sudden attack, fired over his head.

Stubby was laying down a deadly barrage. It was a battle, as in a war. The odds were too great, Sam thought.

Then there was a wild cry and a rider came from the rear of Duffy's people, and men turned and were shot down. . . .

Fawcett Gold Medal Books
by William R. Cox:

CEMETERY JONES

CEMETERY JONES AND THE MAVERICK KID

CEMETERY JONES AND THE MAVERICK KID

William R. Cox

FAWCETT GOLD MEDAL • NEW YORK

A Fawcett Gold Medal Book
Published by Ballantine Books
Copyright © 1986 by William R. Cox

Library of Congress Catalog Card Number: 86-91186

ISBN 0-449-12905-5

Manufactured in the United States of America

First Edition: November 1986

Samuel Hornblow Jones sat on the veranda of El Sol Saloon, boots outstretched, resting in the afternoon shade. The pleasant valley town of Sunrise lay stretched out before him, with people going about their business in leisurely fashion. It was springtime and every prospect pleased the eye.

Inside, Renee Hart played Beethoven, one of the opuses, he could never get the numbers straight. He enjoyed music, but there was, he had discovered, something a bit wrong with his ear; he could not distinguish the finer points but only responded to rhythms and melodies. He did, however, certainly respond to the handsome Renee Hart.

It was a time of contentment, of peace. He admired his boots, handmade in El Paso by a Mexican artist, suitable for both walking and riding, not cowboy footgear but those of a well-to-do citizen, soft and comfortable. He had, he admitted, become somewhat of a dude, what with Renee choosing his wardrobe and having time on his hands. Only the Colt .44 at his side was a remembrance of other times. Without it he would have felt naked. A boy and his dog went trotting by, yelling, "Hey, Sam!" waving, grinning.

"Go get 'em, Dink." Sam knew everybody in town. He was by all standards a settled citizen, a man of means. He had never thought of such a circumstance coming to pass, having been for the main part too busy at this and that before now.

Marshal Donkey Donovan, youthful, scrubbed, and neatly attired, rode in and waved as he made his way to the livery stable. Sam had been his sponsor after the death of old Dick Land. Donkey was part of the warp and woof of Sunrise.

Farmer Edison drove his hay wagon in and pulled up at the establishment of Mayor Wagner: Hay, Grain and Feed. Down the street little Dink hooted and suddenly dove from the street to the boardwalk. Two riders were coming, charging in too fast, throwing up clouds of dust behind them.

Sam half rose, peering. The first rider entered town, bending low. The second drew a rifle from its scabbard. The shot rang clear in the afternoon air.

The first rider went down, sideways to the right, his foot caught in the stirrup. The rider who had fired pulled up, endeavoring to turn his horse and make a run for it.

It was a long shot, but Sam did not think twice about it. The Colt came automatically into play; he seemed not even to aim.

The second rider threw up his arms. He bent double, then dove from the saddle and lay in the road, unmoving.

"Head shot," muttered Sam. "Damn. Could've asked that jasper some questions. Gettin' out of practice loafin' around town."

Suddenly Main Street was full of people. They ran to catch the horses of the two riders; they ran to the prone bodies. Renee Hart come out and put her hand on Sam's shoulder even as he automatically reloaded his revolver. She was a tall woman with wide shoulders, always dressed in long gowns made far away from Sunrise. Her dark hair was drawn back over shapely ears to hang loose in waves. Her large onyx eyes rested sadly upon the scene.

She said, "Did you have to do it, Sam? Did you have to?"

"Could've dropped the horse," Sam confessed. "Shoulda, in fact. Thing is, the horse didn't shoot anybody."

Donkey Donovan was kneeling by the first victim. He looked up, beckoned to Sam. "Man's callin' your name."

Sam walked to the spot where a sunburned, creased face stared up at him. "You Charlie Downs?" he asked.

The man said, "Was . . . Stubby Stone . . . sent me. . ." The man half smiled and died.

"Stone a friend of yours?" asked Donkey Donovan.

"One time. Long ago. Didn't turn out good," said Sam.

Dr. Oliver Bader came up to them with his black bag. He was more sober than usual. He shook his head and asked, "How about the other one?"

"Might's well get Jim Spade for 'em both," Sam told him.

Spot Freygang was running, struggling with his bulky camera equipment, and calling, "Lemme get them. Lemme get the whole scene. The paper comes out tomorrow."

"One thing about Spot," the doctor said. "He's always on the job. Necrophilia of a sort."

"Whatever that means." Sam was staring down at Charlie Downs. Memories were flooding him, mainly unpleasant. The peace and quiet of Sunrise had been cracked like a broken mirror all within a very few moments. He went back to where Renee waited. People ran to help Jim Spade carry the dead men to his undertaking establishment. Under Marshal Donovan's directions, it became an orderly process despite the interference of Spot Freygang and his camera. Little Dink, white-faced, ran to his mother, the dog at his heels. Mayor Wagner came out of the saloon where he had been playing cards.

"Never can have an afternoon of peace and quiet. I'd better check with Donkey." He went hurrying off.

Renee asked, "What about the man you shot, Sam?"

"What about him? Donkey will learn what needs to be known. What I need is a drink."

She led the way into the bar. It was a nice, clean place, well run by Casey Robinson, with a long mahogany bar, back mirror, rows of bottles and shiny glasses, and lit by high chandeliers. Casey returned from the veranda and put out a bottle of the best. Sam poured four ounces and drank it neat. Renee went to the piano and played something from Bach, very solemn, not for the first time in relation to death in the environs of Sunrise.

Sam thought about Charlie Downs, cowboy, and Stubby Stone, who had once been his friend and partner and then had been not so friendly. There was still an unpaid debt to Stubby, the rascal; he had once saved Sam's life in a cross-fire. Whatever else had passed between them, that remained a debt to be paid off.

Sam went to the piano with a second drink. He listened to the music, watching Renee's long, slender, lovely hands. The piece fitted his mood, and she knew it. She knew all she needed to know about Sam "Cemetery" Jones.

To others, many others, he had been a cattleman, a lawman, a professional gambler, a miner, but never a thief. At fourteen, he had gone up the cattle trails learning that hard work at low pay did not suffice for him. He had seen the towns settle and grow, as Sunrise had, noted the changes as civilization had reached out tendrils into the West. He had known the Indians and watched what happened to them when they'd attempted to preserve their way of life. He had come to certain decisions. His character had been molded under duress, and he hated the cognomen "Cemetery" yet knew he had earned it.

Quick hands—he had always had the quick hands plus a certain sense of self-protection that kept him alive. His was not an impressive figure, lean and long and wiry rather than bulky. He was not a devout lover of horses, though he recognized good horseflesh and knew when and where to hire it. He knew the West, knew its denizens, and he was willing under any circumstances to face facts, however ugly. There was about him an aura of mystery.

Now Donkey Donovan came to him in El Sol. The young marshal was a solemn, steady, tanned ex-cowboy who took his position seriously; he was brave and stubborn and loyal. He had a crumpled piece of paper in his hand, which he proffered. "I found this on the fella you called Downs. It's for you."

Sam held the paper to the light of a chandelier and read aloud:

Sam:
Need you bad. The ranch. They got me in a bind. Mary sends her best.
Stubby

"So the chickens came home to roost," said Sam, half to himself.

"We rounded up the horses. Fella you shot rode D Bar D. T'other is Crooked S," Donkey said.

"That figures," Sam said. "Crooked S is Stubby Stone's brand."

"No posters out on either of 'em."

"Wouldn't be. Just a couple of rannies working for their bosses," Sam said. "From down Texas."

"Anyone to notify?" asked Donkey.

"I'll attend to it."

"Okay. See you later." The marshal departed.

Renee Hart asked, "Upstairs, Sam?" She knew his every mood. He followed her to her room on the second story of El Sol.

It was a spacious room for a special lady. It was furnished with a taste and sensibility bred far from Sunrise, in the old city of Philadelphia from whence Renee originated. There was a Homer Winslow on the wall, bright curtains, a large comfortable bed covered with a thick handmade quilt, two deep chairs upholstered in velvet, walnut chests, and a huge closet for her many gowns. Every so often she rearranged or redecorated in part. There were two large windows, one of which the owner, Casey Robinson, had caused to be cut through for her.

Renee sank into a chair, crossed her long legs, and said, "Tell me."

"It was quite a way back," Sam said. "Stubby and I, we had business together. A saloon, gambling, whatever."

"Dancing girls."

"Part of the business. We were interested in branchin' out. Bought a little old ranch, put some beef on it. There was this girl named Mary Malone."

"There would be." Renee smiled at him.

"Well, like I said, it was a while ago and we were pretty young."

"And randy."

"Be kinda sick if we weren't." Sam returned her grin. He was relaxed now. She could always do that for him. "Mary was a good gal. Her folks had been killed by Comanches. She was the dressmaker in town. What happened was, Stubby ran a whizzer on me. Another gal, worked in the saloon, she was in on it."

"I get the picture."

"Yeah, well, I fell for it, Mary married Stubby and I cut out. Didn't know for sure what Stubby had done until I met the saloon gal again later on. Wasn't worth doin' anything about it by then."

"Nor earlier," Renee pointed out. "You were guilty, were you not?"

"Yeah. Besides, Stubby had saved my life."

"I see."

"Two gunners had me in a crossfire and he cut in."

"So now you owe him. In your fashion."

"Why, there's no other way," Sam said.

"Right. Where is this place and when do you leave?"

"It's down on the Pecos. Town called Bowville. The Crooked S is a few miles south. Good range, farmin', mountains." He paused. "Maybe tomorrow."

"Yes. Two people dead. Morning stage?"

"Could be." She never held him back for a moment. If he hadn't known her so well, he might have thought she didn't care, wouldn't miss him. "I'll make it as quick as can be."

"If you live through it."

"I generally manage."

She shook her head ever so slightly. "It's still wild country, Sam. You've been on the edge so many times. Sometimes I wonder: Is it worth risking your life at the drop of a sombrero?"

"You still don't talk western real good," he said. "More like drop of a Stetson."

"Sombrero," she insisted. "You do the Mexican hat dance around danger, darling."

"Not because I want it thataway."

"I know. I know. The code. The tradition." She shook her head. "It's what must be, that is true."

"No use argufyin' on it." Sometimes he deliberately used the common language, although he had learned better from her. It never failed to amuse her. She seemed closer to him then. He needed her now. Killing a man offhand had brought back to him the hated nickname "Cemetery" Jones. He did not want the world to know what went on in his gut at those times.

"I think we shall have food," she said. "I think we shall have drink. I know we shall have music. I hope we shall have love this night."

"Yes, ma'am." He arose and bowed low.

She came to him and they held each other with the utmost tenderness.

2

The driver of the stage was an old-timer. He handled the ribbons of six horses with consummate ease and his tongue ran with the cadence of the hoofs. "You heard about Pecos Bill? How his family done lost him in Texas and he was raised by coyotes and grew so mean the rattlers used to hide when they heard him comin'?"

"I heard," Sam said. He was bone-weary from riding the stage. He was up on the box to avoid the gab of a drunken drummer and a woman of some avoirdupois, who reeked of cheap perfume.

"Used mountain lions for saddle horses. Didn't have no pets, so he invented scorpions."

"I heard."

"Pecos Bill, he was a Texican."

"I heard." Sam had asked only if there was a stage between Pecos and Bowville.

"Ain't no stage to Bowville," the driver said.

It was just as well. One more ride in a Concord or atop one and he would be jostled to death—or bored to pieces.

"Heard there was trouble down Bowville way," the driver went on. "Them ranchers, they're always feudin' and fussin'. Not that Pecos ain't a tough burg. You know Pecos?"

"Long time ago," said Sam. He hoped nobody in town remembered him. He would have to buy a horse, he supposed; renting would be risky—for the horse. Pecos had grown, he knew, since the days when he had walked its boardwalks and dealt with the toughest of the tough. It had become the seat of operations for farmers and ranchers since then and had probably calmed down a bit. There was still the saying, "No law west of the Pecos," which meant the river, and Bowville was indeed west of the one-hundred-and-thirty-mile stream.

The driver maundered on about the town of Pecos and all the bad men and gals he had known there over the years until they came down the main street and he cracked his whip before pulling up at the stage station. Sam gathered his bedroll and his rifle and swung down, his bones creaking. He looked up at the driver and said, "You never did tell me how Pecos Bill mounted a cyclone and traveled over three states levelin' mountains and uprootin' forests. That's how come we've got the Panhandle. Bill never would've stopped if the cyclone hadn't rained out on him."

Leaving the old man agape, Sam limped toward the Pecos House and registered. He went immediately to his room, then found a youth on duty and ordered hot water for a bath. He had never been more in need of a decent meal, especially after those served at stage stops. One more day of that kind of travel and he'd no doubt wish Stubby had forgotten his name.

After an hour, it was still daylight and he felt better. He gave the boy his laundry to be done that night, paid in advance with a generous tip, and went down to the lobby. It was a first-class hostelry, with a buxom lady behind the desk. She told him, whispering conspiratorially, that the best food was not served on the premises but down the street at Josie's Eatery. Sam often had that effect on women, of which he was well aware and never hesitated to utilize.

Josie turned out to be the sister of the hotel lady and the food was indifferent, but since Sam was ravenous, the meal sufficed. It was still daylight when he left to find the livery stable. There he met a character named Buffalo Willy who tried to sell him two broken-down beasts before he admitted to owning a big roan called Junior that he might sell for a price. Sam wearily bargained and finally, after a close examination and a walk around in the yard with the animal, parted with fifty dollars and another fifty for saddle and bridle and blanket.

Buffalo Willy, who had a goatee and long hair, asked him where he was from.

"Up north," said Sam.

"Goin' south?"

"Thereabouts."

"Bowville?"

"Maybe." There was obviously a reason behind the man's curiosity.

"Hired out to Duffy?"

"Don't know any Duffy."

"You're wearin' that gun low and tied down." Buffalo Willy cackled.

"This Duffy is hiring gunners?"

"You get to Bowville you'll learn."

"Could be." Sam departed, walking back toward the hotel. It was now dusk. There were few people in the streets. In an alley near the hotel, there was a scuffle going on. Kids were fighting in a pack. A couple of passersby stopped to cheer them on. Pecos was still that kind of town. Sam took a look.

There seemed to be three boys attacking each other. Then Sam perceived that two of them were working on one, a small, skinny kid who swung both hands and an occasional foot. Still, there could be no doubt of the outcome. One of the pair kicked the lone kid in the shins. The little one winced but did not cry out. It was then that Sam decided to take a hand. He grabbed the attacking pair and held them at arm's length. He said, "Can't fight fair nohow, huh?" He shook them, swung them around, and pitched them into the street. One of the bystanders said, "Hey, you got no cause buttin' in."

Sam stared and asked, "You want any part of it?"

The man started to speak, looked into Sam's eyes, and shook his head, then walked away muttering to himself. Sam turned to look for the little kid he had protected. All he saw were flying legs going around the corner at the far end of the alley. He shrugged and strolled on to the hotel. Crossing the lobby to the stairway, he glanced out the window.

Framed in a pane of glass was a face. The eyes were large and round and widely spaced. The hair was straggly, dark brown, probably dirty. The mouth was a slit, rather small. The chin was firm. It was a white face that might well denote hunger. He paused, about to go back outdoors. The face vanished in a flash.

He looked after the flying, small figure and recognized it as that of the kid from the alley fight. He was too weary to follow.

He went upstairs and to bed. He slept like the proverbial log.

In the morning Sam ate breakfast at the hotel—he figured it was impossible to ruin eggs and bacon and proved himself wrong—then went down to the livery stable and saddled up Junior, the roan. Buffalo Willy waved him good-bye, calling, "Duffy pays good but he's a sumbitch."

Sam rode the remembered road to Bowville, which was no main highway. It was rutted and dusty. It led through rich country. Oaks and pines grew willy-nilly; wildflowers bloomed where man had not applied himself to industry. He passed several farms and a small ranch.

The roan was tractable and had an easy gait. A small animal scuttled across the road and Junior shied but did not buck, calmed by Sam's reassuring voice. It was a sunny day, pleasant enough for a ride in the country.

He came to where the road meandered away from the Pecos River, past a clump of alders he did not remember. The sun was high. He tugged at his hat brim to keep it out of his eyes.

Three men with drawn guns rode out of the trees. They effectively blocked the narrow road. Sam reined in and waited.

The one who seemed to be the leader was clean-shaven but had not lately used his razor. He wore range clothing that was none too clean. The others seemed sharper; they had the eyes Sam had so often noted in gunslingers, unblinking and watchful.

"Where you goin', stranger?" asked the leader.

"None of your damn business," said Sam calmly.

"We're makin' it our business. You savvy?"

"So?"

The man was a bit confused. "So, we wanna know who you are, see? And where you're bound for."

"You heard me." Sam was wondering which one to take out first if he had to make his move. The leader was a straw boss perhaps, certainly the least threatening. The man on the right with a scar staining his upper lip might be the most dangerous. The third man did not look much easier.

"You're on the property of Mr. Duffy," said the interrogator. "We got a right to ask."

"Don't know any Mr. Duffy," Sam replied. He shifted with great care so that his right hand was free to reach for the Colt.

One of the other riders said, "Take it easy, mister."

"No hurry." He was strangely relaxed, yet it was not so strange—it was a situation he had experienced before. A bird sang in the trees beyond and to the right of the riders. What had Renee said? "If you live through it . . . You've been on the edge so many times." So here it was, the edge of death again. He could not back down; it was simply not in him.

The leader said, "We don't take no razzledazzle from nobody, mister. No one gets through here without tellin' who he is and what's his business."

Sam said, "That right? Nobody?"

"You heard me."

"Then what about that gun behind you?"

Only the leader turned to look. In that instant, Sam had his gun in his hand and was covering the trio.

"Don't believe me?" he asked. "Take your time."

A gun went off. Dirt kicked up very near the three riders.

Now the other two whirled in their saddles. They were experienced, so they did not go for their weapons.

On the edge of the road, near the trees, stood a small figure. The thin kid held a shotgun in his hands. It was pointed in their general direction.

"Makes you stop and think, don't it?" Sam said. He recognized the kid, of course. The face was still white, but the mouth had turned hard and the eyes shone.

Sam went on. "If I was you boys, I'd skedaddle. Know what I mean? Just keep goin' in whatever direction you came from and don't look back." He holstered his revolver and drew the .44 rifle from its scabbard.

The dark rider said, "Man knows what he's talkin' about."

"A damn button," complained the blond man. "C'mon, Simon, you damn fool."

"A damn, skinny, little ol' kid," said Simon.

"He's got another barrel to that thing," said the dark

man. "Further and more, I don't like the look o' this strange jasper."

Simon said, "I'll ketch holy hell over this." He turned his horse around. All three rode back up the road.

"See you again, stranger," one of them threw back over his shoulder; then they were gone around the bend in the road.

Sam put his rifle back in its place and looked down at the boy, who was reloading his shotgun with professional dexterity. "How did you get out here so quick, youngster?"

"Didn't walk." It was a musical though husky voice. "You best follow me. They'll be layin' for you."

"How do you know where I'm headed?"

"If you ain't for Duffy, you're for Stone," said the kid.

"You a friend of Stubby?"

"I'm nobody's friend. I look out for me." The round face turned to ivory, cold as marble. "You took up for me last night. I can lead you round about to the Crooked S."

"What's your name, sonny?" Sam was never quite comfortable with children. This one was patently more difficult than any he had ever encountered before.

"Mac."

"Mac what?"

"Just plain Mac." The chin still had that stubborn set, the unwinking eyes did not change expression. The kid wore a loose linsey shirt, a pair of greasy-looking buckskin pants, moccasins, and a buckskin vest sizes too large. His hat was a battered flattop with a narrow brim. The picture as a whole was not prepossessing, yet there was an alertness, a grace when he moved toward the trees that transcended the shabbiness. Sam walked the roan into the clump of alders, which joined a stand of oak and other varieties and became a stretch of forest. There was a clearing and in it stood a wiry mustang wearing a beat-up cavalry saddle. There was a bedroll in place, and on the ground was a package. The kid called Mac opened the package and took out hardtack and jerky, motioning for Sam to join him.

"No, thanks," Sam said, swinging down, trailing his reins. "You live around here?"

"Yep." The boy was nibbling at the food, staring hard at Sam.

"Whereabouts?"

"All over."

"Where's your folks?"

The kid shook his head. He continued to regard Sam with his large dark eyes. "You're Cemetery Jones."

"I don't cotton to 'Cemetery.' Sam's more to my liking."

"I know. Sam Jones. Used to be with Stubby Stone."

"You're too young to remember that."

"Yep."

"How do you know so much?"

"I listen."

Sam considered. "So you've no folks, no home?"

"I get along."

"Just scroungin' around?"

"Call it whatever you like."

"Because of what happened yesterday you hustled out here figurin' I'm on my way to see Stubby Stone, right?"

"Whatever you say."

This wasn't going as it should. Sam waited. Nothing was forthcoming, he found, just that unblinking stare. He finally said, "I could loan you some money to get fixed up. Buy you some cartridges. A meal in town."

"No, thanks."

Again the silence. A bird caroled; one by one others joined in. The kid scattered crumbs, carefully folded up the paper sack, and stored it in a saddlebag. In a graceful leap, he mounted the mustang. "Best to follow me. Narrow trail."

There seemed to be no other course. It was not really a trail, merely a path through brush, sometimes running tightly between trees, but the kid knew every inch of it. He had probably made it himself, Sam thought. He had noted what seemed to be a sheathed machete dangling from the pommel of the kid's saddle. That would account for the shorn brush at occasional spots along the way. This was a mysterious kid, all right, and Sam had made no inroads in the mystery.

He called out and the kid stopped. He asked, "Back yonder, somethin' puzzled me. Fella said I was on Duffy's property."

"Duffy bought up there."

"I thought he had a ranch down by the Crooked S."

"He does."

"This Duffy, he's spreadin' out a heap, seems like."

"Right." The monosyllable was cold as ice.

"You know him?"

Thin shoulders shrugged, then the kid pointed ahead. "Right through there and you're on the edge of Bowville."

"Comin' along? Buy you a meal at least."

"I got other business."

"You're a funny kid. Seems like I could maybe do somethin' for you if you'd pay heed."

"I appreciate it," said the boy, and his voice sounded thinner, even more melodious. "Got to do it my own way."

"Do what?"

The shaggy head wagged. The mustang swung about and the boy was gone back into the woods. There was no sense following, Sam thought. In the first place, he could get lost trying to keep track of the flying mustang and its rider. In the second place, it was like getting blood out of a stone to extract anything informative from the lad. Somehow he had a notion that they would meet again. He rode on.

Bowville had changed some. There was a small park in its center, and a new street ran east and west to match the old main stem running slantwise northwest by southeast. There was also a new hotel. Sam put his horse up at a convenient stable and carried his bundle to the hotel. He registered, unwilling to ride to Stubby Stone's ranch after dark. The clerk advised him to eat at Antonio's Cafe.

Following his directions, he walked along the main stem. The streets were busy with swaggering cowboys, townspeople, a couple of farmers, teamsters from a freight train up at the edge of town, dogs, women in sunbonnets, a couple of giggling teenage girls, and kids swaggering in imitation of their elders. The men still wore guns, he noted, glad that he had neglected to leave his at the hotel.

He found Antonio's Cafe, which was empty of customers at this early hour, and took a table near the window. A stout man with a bandito's mustache, an apron around his ample middle, came from the kitchen and said, "Ain't ready for supper."

"Clerk at the hotel sent me," said Sam. "I'm hungry for a decent steak, scrambled eggs, mashed potatoes, and whatever. Beer, too, if it's cold."

The man took a second look, cocking his head to one side. He said, "Don't I know you?"

"That don't matter, does it? I'm here for food."

"I was a swamper across the street."

Across the street was the saloon once owned by Sam and Stubby Stone. A sign now read DUFFY'S PLACE. Sam squinted at the man. "There was a skinny kid. Called him 'Tony get to work, damn you'."

"That was me. Stubby loaned me enough to get my start here."

"Do tell." Stubby had a generous streak, especially after a lucky day at the tables.

"I remember when the gambler said your wheel was crooked and he had a cover gun and Stubby cut in. Saved your bacon. You're Sam Jones."

Sam said, "Then you do know me."

"I put on a little weight since then. Stubby—he didn't do so good."

The sign on the saloon across the way was professionally painted; the building was in good repair; men went in and came out. It seemed to be doing very well.

"You put on a lot of weight. So Stubby sold the joint."

Antonio shook his head. "Pat Duffy, he crooked him out of it."

"Do tell."

"Poker game. I seen it all. Duffy brought in a dealer."

"Didn't need a dealer. Stubby never did know how to play poker," Sam said.

"They did it neat. Stubby had an aces full. Four treys beat his ass."

"Sloppy."

"So Stubby and his wife, they went out to the ranch."

"So that's the way it was." Sam shrugged. "How about my supper?"

Antonio raised his voice. "You heard the man. Give him the best we got." He said to Sam, "I knew Stubby was took, but there was nothin' to do about it. Duffy already had guns; he'd bought the marshal. All that."

"Who's Duffy?"

"Came in from Mexico. Gold, he had gold. Bought the spread next to Stubby's, y'know? On the river? 'Course you know."

"I know." The picture was clear except for one aspect. "You mean Stubby hasn't got men?"

"Some. Charlie Downs."

"Forget him."

Antonio nodded. "He's been gone awhile."

"He's gone for good."

Antonio stroked his mustache. "He wasn't much."

"He was alive."

"Sam Jones. Okay. Me, I mind my own business, y'know? But if I can do anything . . ."

"You already did."

A customer opened the door, and Antonio moved fast for a fat man, saying, "Best we don't know each other." He went to the kitchen as the customer took a seat across the room, staring at Sam.

The activity in the street continued. Sam watched Duffy's Place. It continued to fill up. Duffy was doing a land-office business. Sam wondered if he was in town, this Pat Duffy.

The meal came: a thick, juicy steak, lightly scrambled eggs, a bowl of mashed potatoes with gravy on the side, and a platter of biscuits with butter and honey, plus a steaming cup of coffee and an icy-cold bottle of beer. It seemed that Antonio knew his business.

The other customer rose and went to the kitchen door, spurs clanking. He was lean, tanned, weatherworn. He said, "I'll have what the man is havin'."

Antonio's voice came faintly "Ain't suppertime. The man's a special customer."

The stranger stepped inside the kitchen and said something Sam could not hear. Then he recrossed the room and stood looking down at Sam. "Excuse me, sir, but I'm a stranger in town. Mind if I join you?"

There was a very small shield on his vest. Sam asked, "You the marshal?"

"Ranger."

"Set yourself." Texas Rangers were not to be ignored under any circumstances, Sam knew.

"Had a hard ride down from Pecos," said the Ranger. "Name of Keen."

"Sam Jones."

"Pleased."

The conversation seemed to be at a standstill. Then Sam asked, "Any of my business what's happening?"

"Maybe. You heard anything about a range war?"

"Somethin'. Has to do with a man named Duffy?"

"And one by the name of Stone."

Sam nodded at the establishment across the street. "Duffy seems to do right well by himself."

"I'm findin' that out. Don't take but a question or two around town."

"You checked out the saloon yet?"

"I like to fill my stomach before I drink." The lean face could smile easily and pleasantly.

"Me, too."

The Ranger rubbed a thumb across his upper lip. "Sam Jones. You're not wearin' your badge."

"I retired." The Rangers always knew too much. There were not many of them, but they had hundreds of friends.

"Sunrise, up north. Outlaws. The Colemans. Rob Pitman."

"Yup." There was no use denying it. It had all been in the *Sunrise Enterprise*, thanks to Spot Freygang, reporter and photographer of dead men.

"They rebuilding the town?"

"Yup." The least said the better. Sam ate the good food.

"Mean bunch you cleaned up."

"The meanest." Sam added, "Not me. The town."

"We heard. You down here to see Stubby Stone?"

The pleasant Ranger knew altogether too much. Sam said, "Possibly."

"We sorta keep track of things here in Texas," said Keen, still smiling. "Range wars, barbed wire, none of our business. Until somebody get hisself killed."

"Way I hear it—range war or riot, one murder—one ranger."

"They do say." Keen shrugged. "Ain't many of us. Big damn state, Texas."

"Yup."

Antonio brought over an identical meal to Keen. Sam said, "Antonio, put up some decent grub for me, please?"

The fat man whisked an apple pie out from under his apron. "On the house. Savvy?"

They both said, "Thanks."

Antonio said, "Trouble comin'. I got to stay out, understand?"

The door slammed open, and Antonio turned toward it, resigned, hands folded beneath the apron. A big man entered. He wore a Spanish-style flat hat beneath which graying hair showed, a short jacket, and tight black trousers. He had long, strong legs and arms. On his pug-nosed, rubicund face was, Sam noted, "the map of Ireland." He had hard blue eyes, a wide mouth, clean-shaven pink skin, and a slightly prognathous jaw. Close behind him were two flashy saloon girls and the three men Sam had encountered on the road.

The man called Simon said excitedly, "I told ya. That's him. That's the smartass."

"Please, Mr. Duffy, no fighting in here. My furniture, my kitchen," pleaded Antonio. He need not have given the tip-off as to the identity of Pat Duffy, Sam thought, but it was a generous thought.

Duffy stomped across the board floor on black boots with heels that made him appear even taller than his natural height. He stood behind Keen and stared down at Sam.

"You the hombre who rousted my men?"

"Who are you?" Sam did not stop eating; his voice was mild.

"I'm Pat Duffy."

Sam shook his head. "Cuts no ice with me."

"That was my land you was on, me buckaroo." There was a trace of brogue in Duffy's intonation.

"That was a public road," Sam said, his voice growing colder.

"I wanna know who comes my way," said Duffy. "I got property to protect. You understand, me buckaroo?"

In the background, the girls giggled; Simon stood hunched; the blond gunman and the dark-haired one spread apart. Keen sat with bent shoulders concealing his tiny badge and grinned at Sam. Antonio retreated to the kitchen door.

Sam sighed, then leaned back and looked up at Duffy. "In the first place, I ain't your buckaroo. In the second place, I don't like the way you come at a fella. In the third place, I don't think you or your mob, there, are tough enough to do anything about me or my ways. You savvy, me Irish spalpeen?"

For a moment it seemed Duffy would swell up and burst on the spot. The veins in his neck stood out like whipcord. His face turned fiery red. As he began to roar, Keen suddenly stood up and faced him, still grinning.

Keen said, "Seems to me you got a problem here, Mr. Duffy."

Light caught the Ranger badge. Duffy blinked. His choler diminished, little by little. He seemed to dwindle an inch or so. He swallowed. He managed a sickly grin.

"Texas Ranger, is it, now? A friend of this, uh, gent?"

"We're acquainted."

"He a Ranger, too?"

"Nope. He's a man entitled to travel the public road. Like he says."

"Well . . . I see what you mean, Ranger." Duffy was a man who knew which side his bread was buttered on. "However, I have been threatened. There's a problem, y'see. Nothing the law would be interested in. Just . . . problems."

"We've heard," said Keen.

"Ye can't believe all ye hear, now can ye?" Duffy essayed a laugh. "It's a small thing, for true."

Sam was looking out the window, allowing the Ranger to carry on. Again he saw the white face of the urchin amidst a crowd of curious onlookers who had followed

Duffy and his coterie. As soon as he made eye contact, the kid vanished into the background.

"There's a man missing," said Keen. "Name of Charlie Downs. People have been asking for him."

Sam said, "Charlie Downs is dead up in Sunrise."

"That's one of Stubby Stone's men," said Duffy virtuously.

"One of your men is also missing," Keen said. "Name of Buck Tinsley."

Sam told them, "Tinsley died after he shot Charlie Downs. Up in Sunrise." It had to come out in the open, and this seemed as good a time as any with the Ranger present. "Glad to know Tinsley's name. For the headstone on Boot Hill."

"So you're Cemetery Jones!" The words burst, uncontrolled, from Pat Duffy.

The gunmen now froze. Simon's eyes rolled. Keen stepped back, giving himself elbow room.

Sam said, "People don't call me that to my face more'n once." He shoved back his chair. Everyone jumped a trifle. The girls squeaked and edged toward the exit.

Pat Duffy swallowed. "Uh, no offense."

"You seem to have knowledge of how come Downs and Tinsley were out of town," said Keen, shaking his head. "Knew Mr. Jones had something to do with their whereabouts. That's not what you indicated."

Duffy visibly pulled himself together. His natural color returned, and his voice lowered, more under control. "If you gentlemen have got anything to charge me with, tell me."

Keen said, "If there was a charge, I wouldn't be standin' here jawin' with you, Mr. Duffy. Mr. Jones is not at present a lawman. If I were you, I'd go about my business. Easy-like."

Duffy seemed about to speak, then smiled thinly and

waved a hand. The girls, the gunners, and Simon went out into the street.

Duffy said, "The drinks are on me if you care to partake, gentlemen. Right across the street."

He bowed and followed his little group. Keen sat down and attacked the apple pie. Sam followed suit. Antonio came out of the kitchen and stared out the window as the crowd dispersed.

"Hope they don't come back for supper," he said.

"I reckon they'll lay low for a bit," said Keen. "We had a sorta wet-blanket effect on 'em, wouldn't you say?"

"He's got a bug in his ear, all right," Sam said. "He knows that I'm on to the fact he sent Tinsley after Downs. Maybe he don't know Downs was carryin' a message for me. He can guess that, though, seein' I'm here."

"Stone sent for help?"

"Yup."

"Stone is no little blue wildflower."

"No."

Keen looked off for a moment. Then he said, "I've been with the Rangers a long while, and my pappy before me. Seems there was a rangdoodle in Bowville. Seems like you owe Stubby Stone."

"Could be."

"Too bad."

"Pardon?"

"I was kinda hopin' we could swing in together."

"You mean together—but separate," Sam said.

"Somethin' like that."

"Still might do."

"Doubtful. You'll excuse me, but you *are* Cemetery Jones. I got a captain; he's persnickety. You're a real sudden man."

Sam shook his head. "It's a cross to bear, friend. They hang a name on you."

"I saw how cool you were just now." There was true

sympathy in the man's voice. "I know those jaspers—Jackson, the yella-haired one; Magrew, the most dangerous. Simon, he's the goat, kisses Duffy's behind, which needs a lot of kissin', I figure. There's a passel of hard cases on Duffy's spread. Stone can't fight 'em nohow. Duffy 'bout owns the town. Took it over piece by piece. Had a wife, a widow he married for her ranch, they say. Got connections way down in Mexico. That's what we know." He paused for breath. "I hadn't oughta be tellin' you all this, but I like your style."

"I appreciate it," said Sam. He had known or guessed most of it, but every little bit might help. "You met Mrs. Stone?"

"Haven't met her. I've been layin' low as best I could. Nothin' to go on."

"I see. Takes time and patience when you're wearin' a badge."

"True."

"Well, I better be moseyin' along. You finished with the pie?"

"Uh-huh."

Sam took the rest and inserted it in the package of food Antonio had ready for him. He paused beside Keen and said, "It was right good meetin' you."

"Convenient, too." The Ranger's grin reappeared, and they shook hands. *"Hasta la vista."*

Sam went out onto the street but not without taking slanting glances to make certain that the coast was clear. People walked widdershins around him, due no doubt to the scene witnessed by so many who had peered into the restaurant window. He had the frontiersman's instinct that he was being followed—instinct? Suspicion? He was a bit wound up. He carried the parcel of food in his left hand, leaving his right free and near to the butt of the Colt .44.

He entered the hotel and went up the stairs to his room on the second floor, which faced the front. He drew the shade against the light from the street. Dusk was turning into night; Duffy's saloon was loud and bright. Sam removed his shirt and used the water basin, then dumped the water into the chamber pot. He removed his gun belt, took the gun from it, and placed it on the bed before doffing his boots. The door was on a dead bolt. There was an awning below the window, so he opened it at the top, setting a trap with a balanced water tumbler in case of an attempt to enter or even to tamper with the drawn shade. Stretching out on his back, he reviewed the afternoon and evening. The white face of the maverick kid would not go away.

He had been on the frontier at fourteen. He was taller and stronger than the kid who called himself Mac. Sam had carried water, hay, straw—whatever they gave him to tote. He had learned in various and sundry ways to protect himself, always staying within himself, keeping his own counsel. He had gone up the trail with the herds, learning, listening, keeping out from underfoot, practicing with his ever-quick hands as he found out the way to stay alive in the harshness of the West.

He had known Indians, lived with Apaches. He had seen what happened to the Indian tribes, how they were victimized and what vengeance they had taken. He had formed his own hard opinions and had set up his code: Be quiet, be sure, be brave, be loyal. Other men wore notches on their gun butts; Sam wore them on his soul ever since the day the cowboy in Dodge had called him and he had killed the man and two of his kin.

His little song ran through his head. "A man can kill another man/And still be on the level/ But woe and shame will come to him who sells out to the devil."

There was music to the words, his own music. He had a feeling for simple tunes, which reminded him of Renee Hart. This was not a time to think of Renee, whom he loved and who loved him, each in their fashion. They each had a past that they did not care to dwell upon. They needed one another in certain ways, and that was enough for now.

He had for many years thought himself not capable of loving a woman, truly loving, down to his boots. As Renee knew and pointed out, neither of them was ready to settle down into domesticity. Both of them had the past lurking in deep shadows, and neither was anxious to shed light upon that darkness. Thus they loved in the present, for the present. Her music, that strange talent that produced classical sounds he could hear and enjoy but not fully understand, satisfied his craving for he knew not what.

There was a scratching at his door. He came wide awake and picked up his gun. He crossed the room, placed himself alongside the entry, and asked, "Who's there?"

"Me, Mac," came the strange, hoarse little voice.

He opened the door. The kid came into the room like a shadow in the dimness, standing there, looking solemnly at him.

"Now what the hell?" Sam demanded. "How did you get up here?"

"They'll be layin' for you." The kid did not make a move, yet he was, as always, seemingly prepared for flight.

Sam relaxed. "I sort of knowed. Here, on the table. Food."

Mac went to it, sidling over, not taking his eyes off Sam. "Saw you get it from Antonio."

"So eat it."

The kid did so, not in haste as though starving but rather delicately, wiping fingers and chewing slowly. Sam sat on the bed and watched. Silence persisted in the room.

When Mac had finished, he asked, "Can I sleep on the floor?"

"Your pony okay?"

"Where would I be without him?" There seemed never to be a straight answer.

"There's some water left. Wash up and you can crawl in with me if you don't snore or kick around or anything."

"The floor. Maybe a blanket?"

"Whatever you say. You're a wild one, you know that? Sneakin' around like an Apache. Followin' me, ain't you?" Sam said.

"Any harm done?"

"Not the point. Kid like you, there's danger out there."

"I get along."

"I see that. Where are you from and what are you up to, Mac?"

"Come from nowhere. Up to what happens."

"You saved me a razzledazzle back yonder. I'm grateful."

"You just fed me," Mac said.

"Figured you'd be around."

"You want to get to the Crooked S. You're who you are."

"Yup. I'm who I am."

"I'm who I am."

"That Ranger. You know him?"

"Nope."

"But you know why he's hereabouts," Sam asked.

"Who don't? Range war."

"Duffy against Stone."

The kid nodded, finished the last crumb, then went to the basin, washed, wiped his hands. His every move was meticulous; there was feline grace about him. He looked at the bed and Sam peeled off one of the blankets.

"Take off some clothes, be comfortable," Sam urged.

The kid doffed a loose jacket. Articles in the pockets clinked. He made a pillow of it and skillfully folded the blanket across the threshold of the door.

Sam protested, "Hey, you ain't no hound dog, guardin' the portal."

"Don't mean to be. Still, never can tell." The kid's shotgun stood where he had placed it upon entering. He lay down.

"Well, you sure ain't a bundle of laughs," Sam said. "Have a good night."

Sam slipped out of his pants and began to remove his lightweight long johns but hesitated. The kid's wide eyes remained on him. He liked to sleep nude on a warm night, but there was convention to be observed. He crawled beneath the remaining thin blanket.

He said, "Sleep tight, don't let the bedbugs bite."

"Been bit by worse," said the kid. The big eyes did not waver.

"Hangin' around the way you do, anything could bite you to bits." Sam was already sleepy.

There was noise from without but weariness took hold. Sam drifted off thinking of Pat Duffy, that odd Irishman in the unmatched, unbecoming Mexican getup. There was something peculiar about Duffy. He would have to learn just what.

He dreamed of Renee, which was not unusual. He turned, one eye open, still in the maze of slumber. The wide eyes were still upon him. They glistened in the dimness. No wonder, he thought. A maverick kid wandering around, unwilling or unable to talk, to get it out. A handy kid, though, very handy. That was another puzzle to put together.

3

Stubby Stone awoke at dawn. He leaned over and kissed his wife, very softly so as not to rouse her. He slipped into a shirt and jeans and tiptoed downstairs to the kitchen with his boots in his hand. He donned them, then opened the side door and inhaled the brisk air. It would be hot later, but later was a time for worriment. Now all he surveyed was peaceful.

He was a short man, almost as wide as he was tall. His belly was flat and his bowlegs sturdy. His head was rather small, his ears close set, his face perfectly formed, as handsome as a Greek statue's. He was quite blond, his skin clear, his gray eyes narrow and sharp.

He went back into the kitchen and shaved at the sink. He was proud of his good looks, of the attention he paid his appearance. He liked to think it was why he had won Mary.

He thought of Sam Jones then and winced, nicking himself with the razor. It had been a dirty trick to play on a friend, he had never denied it to himself. He had wanted Mary that bad. Now she was pregnant again. She had lost two. She was in her ninth month, and the trouble with Pat Duffy wasn't doing her any good. They weren't getting any younger and they had wanted children right from the start. It didn't seem fair, the way they loved each other.

He returned to the door. Pit Pickens was going into the henhouse to gather eggs. Pit had been with Stubby since the days when he had owned the saloon. No more loyal man ever lived, he reflected. At seventy years old, he was as spry as a youngster and as fast with a gun. Not as fast as Sam, but quicker than Stubby himself was.

He took his gun belt down from a peg and strapped it on. He carried a short-barreled .38 because it was easier to draw, considering his short arms. He wore it high and hated wearing it at all. Were it not for Duffy . . . He went out to greet Pit.

Pickens was the tallest man in the county. He was thin and gnarled and homely. His grin was wide on his tanned, lined face. He said, "The red hen's settin'. Got about two dozen brown ones, though, from them Hampshire reds."

"Browns are good. Bigger yolks."

Pit said, "The boys'll be stirrin'. I better get in the kitchen."

"Seems so." Pit was a great cook, an enormous help to Mary. "You think Sam's comin?" Pit's grin faded. "We could plumb use Sam."

"He'll be along." Stubby had his doubts, though. Sam wasn't one to forget. On the other hand, there had been the shootout. It was a gamble, a flip of the coin. It depended on which seemed more important to him, and Stubby could hold no rancor if it was Mary that Sam counted first.

He turned and surveyed his house. He had built it well, importing stone, using cement and hard wood. He'd had the money then, before he had lost the saloon. He cursed himself again as he did everyday for the gambling fever that had betrayed him. It had been a weakness, and he was paying for it. He was certain he had been hornswoggled, but there was not a shred of evidence to prove it. The full house had been ace high, his best hand of the evening.

Duffy had been so arrogant and Stubby had wanted desperately to take him down a peg. . . . He made himself stop thinking on it.

He had a fine spread. He had a herd of longhorns to drive to the rails; he had milk cows and a garden. The soil along the Pecos River was fertile; he could live here and enjoy life if it wasn't for that damned Duffy and his cow-stealing bunch. He had strung barbed wire, but he hadn't the men to patrol it and any fool with wire cutters could tear it down.

The men came straggling in from the bunkhouse: Carey, Dobey, and Morgan. Patrolling the herd were Francisco and Callahan. There weren't enough of them to make a fight against the gunmen hired by Duffy. They were also young and inexperienced; three older hands had quit when the war loomed. One, Fielder, had gone over to Duffy. That was bad. Fielder, a mealy-mouth from the north, was too well acquainted with the geography and the strengths and weaknesses of the Crooked S.

Stubby went into the big ranch kitchen. Mary was seated at the end of the long table. Pickens was at the stove, which he had started before daylight, busy stirring and ladling. There were plenty of good victuals, and when the men washed and filed in, everything seemed peaceful and in order.

"How you feel this mornin'?" Stubby asked his wife.

"Like yesterday." She had a sweet smile for them all. "Any sign of Sam?"

"Not yet. He'll be here, never you fret."

"Oh, yes," she said calmly. "Sam will be here."

There was no need to reassure Mary. She had faith. She could forgive, possibly even forget. She awoke with a smile each morning, even though she was never comfortable bearing a child. Time had placed its mark on her; ranch life was hard on all women, but she retained a serene attitude. Stubby was sometimes in awe of her.

Ranch life had not been easy on Stubby Stone, either. He preferred the town. He had been happy in his saloon and gambling joint. The ranch had been Sam's idea. Stubby would have liked Sam to stay and run it, but that had been impossible under the circumstances—the shady circumstances. Mary had faith. He pretended, but he was far from sure that Sam would reply to his appeal for help.

There was the sound of a running horse and a shout. Breakfast was abandoned. Stubby ran into the side yard and saw Francisco sliding down from the saddle, his hat missing, blood on his face. Pit swore and went to the young rider.

"They hit us," Francisco said. "They got about thirty head from the south ferry. We chased 'em. I think we nailed one of 'em."

Pit was wiping away the young hand's blood with his kerchief, still cursing. "Damn it, first blood. Allus starts the big war."

There had hitherto been no bloodshed. Forays had been made at night, clashes avoided. Crooked S cattle had been swiftly driven out of reach so that the brand could be altered, and there had been no real proof of the predators.

Stubby said, "Fat's in the fire. Now we got to do somethin'."

If only Sam were here, he thought. It came down to that; they needed Sam Jones.

Sam was following the small figure on the mustang, taking a circuitous route by way of the river to avoid an ambush. It was a clear day and he was rested and in no particular hurry. He was interested mainly in the kid.

He had awakened to find a plate of hot food at his bedside, the kid eating while sitting cross-legged on the floor. "Antonio" was all Mac said.

From then on it had been a matter of following, as he was doing now. There was no question that the little guy knew every inch of the countryside. Also his head was on straight; he could think and decide in a manner that Sam did not doubt. If there was a war on, Mac was on the side of Stubby Stone and particularly against Pat Duffy. The reason behind all this was what Sam wanted to know. There was no use asking questions, he had long since learned. Best to go along, be ready and hope to find answers.

Mac had muttered something about "comin' in around the south forty," which Sam took to mean Stubby's property since they were heading for Stubby's house.

They were leaving the river through a copse of oak when there was the sound of clanking horns and the light drum of cattle hoofs. The kid's mustang spun on a two-bit piece and then was running like the morning breeze. Sam followed.

They came into the open and already Mac was swinging about. His hand went up, and he yelled in his strange, hoarse voice, "Crooked S. Rustlers."

Sam unlimbered the Remington .44 and spurred the roan. In no time at all, he saw an estimated two dozen head of cattle being driven in the wrong direction, away from Stubby's spread.

There seemed to be four riders. He fired a warning shot over the one at drag. The man ducked and howled. The other three cowhands reined in, grabbing for their guns.

The kid came in close, too close, too daring, and fired the shotgun. A horse went down; the cattle began to stomp faster in their awkward way.

Sam sent another shot as near to a rustler's head as he could come without killing the man. Another of them had one arm already hanging useless, blood on his shirtsleeve, from a previous engagement.

Two men now came from the other direction. They fired again and again. The rustlers took off at top speed. Sam rode down to where the steers were milling and watched the thieves making tracks toward Bowville. Then he wheeled the roan and began circling, putting away the rifle and drawing his revolver. The two men who had been dogging the herd went into action, turning the lead beef so that they milled, finally changing direction. Sam made his run—the roan was not a cattle animal so he was satisfied to bring up the rear, watching over his shoulder lest the rustlers re-form and attack.

One of the cowboys came closer and called, "Name of Callahan. I reckon you're Sam Jones."

Sam could now read the Crooked S brand. "Reckon you're right. Should we take these animals home?"

"We were waitin' for the chance," said the cowboy. He was a homely young man with a wide grin. "Those hombres took too many shots at us. Got Francisco. But we hadn't quit."

"That I can see." He looked now for the kid on the mustang. There was no sign of him. Sam stayed on the drag as they drove the little grab of beef back to the south forty of the Crooked S. The stock had been run hard and moved slowly without much spirit, a fortunate matter for the business at hand.

The cowboy said apologetically, "We're real short-handed. Stubby will be plumb glad to see you."

"Glad to be here." That was very near to an untruth, he admitted to himself. Still, he could not have very well been any place else. Duty and honor . . . well, that sort of thing was calling. Now it was a hard fact that blood had been drawn, which signified that a war was imminent.

He did not bother to ascertain the fate of the rustler who had fallen. He had not been around cattle for some time, but he knew the hard rules. A convenient limb of a tree and a lariat around the neck were the due of a man who stole a steer.

The cowboy said, "Here comes Stubby, hackin' like always."

Sam reined in. Stubby had never been a graceful horseman, but he clung to his oversized saddle like a burr. His hat over his ears, he galloped up and came to a sliding stop.

"Sam."

"Stubby." It was bound to be awkward, a meeting like this. They did not attempt to shake hands.

"Charlie got to you."

"Not quite," said Sam.

"He went down?"

"Fella named Tinsley, they say."

"A no-good rat."

"Charlie was no angel," Sam reminded him.

"I know. I know. But he was my no-good." Stubby shook his head. "Damn nice of you to come. You got my note, then?"

"I got it."

"We got big trouble."

"It'll get worse," Sam said.

Stubby nodded, dolorous. "First blood. Look, Sam, let's go on to the house and palaver some. Mary said you'd be along any minute. She'll be glad to see you."

"Be happy to see her." Sam could not keep the stiffness out of his tone.

Stubby turned to his waiting men, who were listening to directions from Pit Pickens. "You all know what to do. Keep your guns loaded."

Pickens rode up on an old hardy mule. "Sam, good to see you. Sorry it hadda be like o' this."

Sam was glad to take Pit's hand. He knew the value of the old man who had remained loyal to Stubby. "You're lookin' right pert."

"Bit of the rheumatiz, lost a few teeth," he said. "Still can get around a mite. You ain't changed much."

"Outside don't count, does it?"

"Nope. I'll stick around with the boys. We need more of 'em, as you can see with one eye."

"Had enough today." Sam paused, then asked, "You know anything about a button calls himself Mac? Feisty little shaver about fourteen? Rides a mustang, knows this country more than good?"

"That's the little bugger raids the henhouse every so often," said Stubby. "Then he'll lay a brace of birds or a pair of rabbits on the doorstep."

"Been around a while," Pickens added.

"Wasn't for him I wouldn't've been around when those rustlers came through," Sam said. "He's been doggin' my footsteps. Thought he might be connected to you somehow. He's no friend of Pat Duffy, I can tell you that."

Stubby said, "Just a maverick kid. Mary wanted me to find him and see if we could do somethin' . . . Mary loves kids." He paused, and then blurted, "She's goin' to have one of her own any time now."

"Hey, that's great." Sam felt a small twinge, then it went away.

"Well. We lost a couple."

"Oh. Hell, that's real bad."

They were riding toward the house. Stubby said, "It was awful hard on her."

"I'm purely sorry."

"Uh, Sam?"

"Never mind." He knew what was coming, and it embarrassed him. He put up a hand. "What's past ain't worth thinkin' on. Took me a while to figure that out, but I know it's damn true." He did not add that there dwelt in Sunrise a lady named Renee. He wondered if he could feel the same about Stubby were it not for Renee.

"Everything would be fine and dandy if it wasn't for that damn Pat Duffy," said Stubby. "Couple of times I near went gunnin' for him. He's a real bastid."

"I met the man," Sam told him.

"You already did?"

"Bit of a problem with his gunners. That maverick kid got into it. That's the strangest kid I ever come across."

"He totes a shotgun and, I wouldn't be surprised, a hidey gun," said Stubby. "He's like a ghostie comin' and goin' in the night."

"He can disappear in the day. Like right now," Sam said.

"He sided you?"

"He sure as hell did."

"And it seems like he's sidin' me."

"Or just his own self." There was still constraint between them, Sam realized. They did not talk of old times, as would two past partners reunited. It was easier to speak of the kid and of present circumstances. They rode through the countryside and Sam noted changes; everything was richer, more luxuriant in the river basin. It was a fine place to settle down and raise a family and find peace and quiet. It was a downright shame that there had to be a serpent.

They came within view of the house. Only the foundation had been built when Sam departed. Now he said, "Did yourself proud, there. Strong as a fort."

"Comanches," said Stubby. "They were raidin'. They're still out there somewhere, they're always somewhere."

"They move on the moon," said Sam. "Seen any lately?"

"A few rovin' bands. They palaver. I give 'em an old cow once in a while."

They went in through the kitchen, as was customary for riders. Mary still sat at the table. A black woman was cleaning up. Mary smiled and said calmly, "Well, Sam."

"Mary." She was different. He was shocked at the change in her. She had been a smooth-faced, innocent girl; now she was a woman like any other rancher's wife.

She said, "Better light and eat, hadn't you?"

Stubby swallowed, then said self-consciously, "Best we should and talk. Got a lot to talk about."

"I'm going to have a baby, did Stubby tell you?" Mary was proud, yet there was a note of trepidation in her. She had already lost two; she was not without worriment, Sam thought. Yet she was serene and he thought that the marriage had been a good one for them both.

Stubby said to the woman, "Matilda, you mind rustlin' up some grub for us?"

Matilda said, "Always do, don't I? Spend my life rustlin' grub. Be better off rustlin' cows."

"That can get you hangin' from a tree," said Stubby.

It wasn't funny, Sam thought, as he remembered seeing black people dangling from ropes for less reason than stealing cattle. The woman, however, grinned and busied herself at the stove.

The time had come to sit down with Mr. and Mrs. Stone and talk. He thought, as always, of Renee and meekly took his place at the long table.

Pat Duffy sat in the office behind his saloon and gambling joint and listened to Simon prattle on. He was smoking a stogie and caressing a large whiskey with a beer chaser. His head was clear and his choler at the boiling point, but he maintained a calm demeanor until the end.

Simon said, "The kid showed again. With that damn Sam Jones."

Duffy exploded. "I want that kid. How many times have I told you bastids I want that kid?"

"He totes a shotgun," whined Simon. "He slips around so you can't put a finger on him."

"I want that kid!" Duffy was apoplectic with rage. "Find me somebody who can bring in that kid!"

"Everybody's tried. You'd think a button like that, it'd be easy. Where'd he come from, anyways?"

"None of your damn business. Just bring that kid to

me.'' Duffy drained the whiskey and swallowed beer. ''I pay good enough to have done what I want done.''

''I warned all the boys. I told 'em. You want the kid alive. I told 'em like you said.''

''Get the hell outa my sight and tell 'em some more. About the cattle, we got time. Stubby Stone ain't a patch on them I've done in before, me boy, believe me. This here Sam Jones, he ain't all that much. Comes down to it, there ain't never been a man who's all that much. What I want, I get. Now go.''

Simon departed in haste. He was a humble man, a go-between, actually a slave, Duffy thought. It was satisfactory to have one of that kind to kick around. It made him feel good. With the others, the fast guns, he had to be a bit more careful.

He was, he prided himself, not a foolishly reckless man. He used his brains. He got what he wanted and he was like the man who said he didn't want everything—just what was adjacent to whatever he possessed. He had, he believed, the fey quality of the Irish, a gift that allowed him to always come out on top.

He had never seen Ireland. His parents had emigrated to Mexico before he was born, had lived there until they were killed by bandits. He had escaped by hiding in a well. He had found a place in the ranks of a guerrilla band under Santos Liberate and had learned to lie and steal and fornicate and always make a profit. He had stolen a gold shipment one night, killed his two companions in crime, and crossed the border in safety without even being suspected.

Seeking a patina of respectability with the gold as his stake he had married the Widow Murgatroyd, a tiny woman who had wasted away under his abuse. When she died, he had moved to Bowville and bought land and swindled Stubby Stone. It had all been very easy.

All, that is, except the Widow Murgatroyd. Her damn

daughter who had run away just because he had petted her a bit, all in the spirit of fun, of course. And the widow had died hard, cursing him, an Irish curse that might have been daunting to a lesser man.

That was in the past, he scolded himself, pouring the good whiskey and calling, "Rita, my love, cold beer. And where is my darlin' Maizie?"

They came in, hips swaying, dressed in low-cut, short-skirted dresses in bright colors, their hair piled high as he liked it. They were always ready, always listening for his call. They were dance-hall girls by courtesy; they were also his slaves. He had always been one for the ladies. It was a prideful matter to him that he was never without one within call.

Rita was blond and bovine, plump on all counts, simpering, and bore the cold beer. Maizie was small and dark and sharp-featured with amazing breasts for one her size. Rita departed; Maizie, at a nod from Duffy, remained. She was the closest he had to a confidante, a good listener, a proven tomb of silence. She had pretty legs but knobby knees, which she crossed, sitting on the table within easy reach of his hands. She had been left to her own devices at an early age, and was wise in the ways of men of all kinds. She was aware that Duffy wanted to talk.

"You heard Simon? Sure and you did. You read a book once, I remember. So did I, a lot of books. A man can get the smarts from readin' books. The Widow Murgatroyd had books. It was about all she had besides a bit of money, poor thing."

"Yes." Maizie had heard this before when Duffy was into the whiskey.

"So now there has been bloodshed and, truth to tell, I am not displeased, my gal. It had to come, ya see; the war. When a man starts on a way of doin' things, he has to know way ahead what might happen. So now we have this trouble and we have men to fight. We may need more men.''

"Cemetery Jones," she said.

"Ah, you know him?"

"By reputation."

"He has that. A reputation. On the contrary, my dear, he is mortal."

"Ain't we all?"

"Very few of us get outa this world alive." He chuckled.

"And none can take it with us." She knew all the rejoinders to his homilies.

"Thus we enjoy it while we can." He patted her knee. "So we stay as long as we can enjoyin' as much as possible."

"Enjoyin'." She made it sound at least neutral. She enjoyed the laudanum he allowed her, not enough to kill, just enough to get through the days, the weeks, the months. She knew how many whores it had killed; still, she needed something. She was a lot above Rita and the others, she felt.

He said in an altered tone, "Darlin', how many know that you've got Indian blood in you?"

She said, "Only you in these parts. You promised."

"I keep my promises. But tell me, who's a gun as fast as that buckaroo Sam Jones?"

"That remains to be seen."

"So. Now there are Comanches, your people, around."

"I've heard." She frowned.

"You had a friend, a buck. What was his name?"

She was silent, brooding. Then she dashed away a tear and said in a monotone, "He's called Soledad."

"Ah. Soledad. Would he be around, now?"

"Maybe."

"Ah, darlin', don't tease the old man, now. You've seen him."

"What good is he to you?"

"The Comanches need cattle for meat, they need guns. So they don't think you're good enough for their fine young chief-to-be. They'll listen if they can gain somethin'. You see?"

"I see." There was no way out. She was damned if she did and damned if she didn't. Besides, it was an excuse to see Soledad.

"Tell 'em they got my support. My men'll warn 'em when it's time. They can come down on Stubby Stone's place with us behind 'em."

"Uh-huh." Her mind was working. She had been without the drug for two days. She was not yet entirely dependent upon it; she could still reason. "They could get killed, too."

"They kill Mexicans, Apaches, whoever. They got to figure to be targets themselves whatever they do. You go out tonight on that horse I gave you."

She said, "Yes."

"The thing about you," he said, beaming, "is that you are smart enough to know the answers. You won't be sorry, Maizie, believe me."

"Thanks." She was already sorry, but she was patient enough to allow him to fondle her while she made plans for a sortie into the land she knew so well.

4

The usually infallible alarm in Sam Jones's head did not go off that morning until all of the cowhands had departed. He had chosen, over protests, to sleep in the bunkhouse. Some small delicacy had kept him from going to bed in the house with Mary and Stubby, a matter of surprise to him as he thought of it now.

It was barely past dawn. The odor of the bunkhouse was that of oiled bridles, leather, and stale men. It had been a long while since he had experienced such an awakening. He donned his clothing and washed up at the pump in the yard. The day promised to be fair, a cloudless sky and the sun beginning its daily round . . . But it was the earth that went in the circle, he had learned from Renee. He had dreamed of a woman, and that woman had been partly Renee and a bit of Mary from the old days. A disconcerting dream. It was the resultant restlessness that had caused him to oversleep, he thought, hastening to the kitchen.

There another old familiar smell greeted his nostrils, that of pancakes as round and flat as the frying pan and baked beans. His stomach turned over once, then accepted the ranch breakfast that Matilda was dealing out to Stubby and Pit Pickens.

"Sleepin' on your shirttail, eh?" The oldster grinned. "Too much city life."

"Reckon that's it," Sam said.

"Thought we'd ride the fence," said Stubby. "Let you see it all."

"Mary okay?" asked Sam politely.

"Sleeps late. Doc says she should, 'count of losin' the others."

"Ah, I see." Mary's baby had become a deep concern. It could have been his, and his life would have been vastly different. And, he told himself severely, he would not have met Renee. He finished the breakfast in silence.

Pit put together some fodder in a sack and went to the yard to help the wounded Francisco with the chores.

Stubby said, "I know how you feel about Mary and the baby and all, but what can we do? Duffy's got a mortal lock on me. I could maybe sell out."

"Not likely," Sam said. "We'll augur somethin' out. You need more men, that's a big one."

"Can't find 'em. That's why I sent for you. Took a lot outa me to do that, Sam."

"Shouldn't've." But he understood. His old feeling for the stout little man was slowly returning. Stubby would do to cross the river with; he was just kind of boyish in some ways. They were the same age, but Sam had always felt older.

They went outdoors. At the corral, Sam said, "You got a prime remuda here. Plenty of good horseflesh."

"We pride ourselves on that," said Stubby. "Pit, he finds 'em."

"You goin' to make a drive, you better have 'em," said Pickens. "We got near a thousand head out and around. Gonna need some hands. Aim to join up with one o' the big outfits. Got to keep up our style."

Sam nodded and roped his roan. Pit made a bundle of his victuals and added a hammer and nails. "We fix the fence, Duffy's hands tear it down. You'd think the Rangers'd turn up.''

"One did." Sam told them about the man named Keen.

"He better watch his ass," said Pickens. "Duffy wouldn't stop at killin' him."

"Duffy might be damn sorry if he did," said Stubby.

"One war, one Ranger. Never did quite believe in that," Pickens said. They saddled up and rode for the boundary of the Crooked S to the east.

They rode past batches of longhorns grazing, stalking around on long legs made to carry them to the faraway railheads. Pit said, "Them's what made Texas great. Afore you boys was born, they ran wild. Big men threw wide loops, smart men found grazin' land, gov'ment or boughten. Cows and men died, but Texas lived high on the hawg. Still does. Farmers are okay, but who needs 'em? Grow your own, keep your powder dry, that was the way it was. A good way. No damn barbed wire, just people and animals."

"There's always more and more people," Sam observed. "They're comin' by the thousand and don't you forget it. Law's comin', too, and I for one'll be glad to see it."

"Law is Duffy around here," said Stubby.

"That's somethin' we got to look into," Sam told him.

There were trees stretching down and lining the Pecos River. There were wildflowers and birds and small animals scurrying; every prospect was pleasing until they came to the barbed wire. Sam rode up and down for a few rods, then said, "One hammer and a bag o' nails won't do it, Pit."

"I damn well know it." Nevertheless, he dismounted and attempted to make repairs in the sagging lines that had been so mangled that a good-size herd could be run through without too much damage to hides.

Stubby said, "Waste o' time. But Pit, he makes work for himself always. That's the way he is."

"Couldn't have a better man." Sam looked past the wrecked fence. "None of Duffy's cows in sight."

He keeps 'em safe, like as though we were gonna raid." Stubby grinned. "Not that we ain't branded a few mavericks when we could."

They rode the length of the fence, down to the river. Then Stubby said, "I better go back. Just can't help worryin', Sam. The doc's due to ride out any day now and I got to be there. You know, to stand by her and all."

"Sartain." Sam was falling back into the old argot. "You go. I'll mosey around."

He caught up with Pickens as the cowman was taking a breather. Pickens said, "Bad enough we got a war. Havin' a baby at the same time, that's hell. We need kids, all right, boys to work the ranch, take the chores off a growed man. But, hell, bornin' 'em ain't like calvin' a cow."

"You're just as loco about the baby as Stubby, Pit; don't run a line on me."

"Oh, sure." Pit took off his hat and mopped his brow with his rebozo. "It's jest the way things turn around. Baby comes, we take the herd up the trail, all's well on God's good earth. Only there's that Duffy."

Sam said, "You know we could go into town and finish the war."

"Yep. Me keepin' 'em off your back while you gun down Duffy. It ain't done that way no more, Sam."

"Could be. I shot Duffy's man up in Sunrise."

"But he shot Charlie."

"That could be arranged in Bowville with a bit of connivin'."

"There's that Ranger. And the local law, all Duffy's," Pit pointed out.

"If Duffy's dead, it all falls down. Thing is, I can't do it."

"You and me both." Pit squinted. "If you was that kind, you'd a done for Stubby away back then."

Sam shook his head. "There's times I been close, Pit. Real close."

"Close don't count except in pitchin' horseshoes," said Pit.

They were silent. Sam thought of the times he had killed, sometimes within a hair of feeling righteous. He thought of the times he had foreborne. He knew Pit was right, he could not go into Bowville and kill Duffy off-hand. There was cause, of course, surely more than he yet knew. But there was not reason enough, not by the way he had taught himself to live.

As for Stubby, even back then Sam had not thought of going after his partner. He had not been forced to go with the whore, it had been his own randy urge. "All's fair in love and war," the old saying went, and Stubby had been unfair but he had also been in love. And Mary had believed, no blame to her, and she had chosen Stubby. And there was the shootout. No, not even in his youth had he wanted to kill Stubby.

The echo of a gunshot startled Sam's musing. He unslung the rifle from its scabbard. Pit was afoot, also reaching for his long gun. Another blast and then there was the drumming of light hoofs and down the line, racing toward the river, came the little mustang with the kid aboard. The kid was flattened down and the pony was flying like the breeze across the river.

Sam calculated the range and without a target sent shots flying into the heavy growth of trees and brush. Pit, kneeling, was doing the same. The pony came sliding in, all four feet braced. Sam reloaded.

"Always trouble. Yours or mine," he said. "What now, kid?"

"Duffy's men. They been chasin' me all mornin'."

"Cowhands?"

"Nope. Simon and a couple new ones."

"Simon, huh?" Pit shook his head. "Had him along to pick you out. What's Duffy got his back so high up about you for?"

The kid just shook his head.

Sam said, "Hunker down, Mac. You had anything to eat?"

Pit said, somewhat abashedly, "I got vittles. Seems like this button's always around and hungry. Eats like a hawg."

"You two go on down the river," Sam said. "I'll make a pasear and see if those hombres are still lookin'."

"No," said the kid. "There's three of 'em, I told you."

"Don't you fret. Git."

The old man said, "C'mon, kid. When Sam says he's goin' to do somethin', you might as well go along with it."

There was a spot where Pit had not repaired the fence. Sam rode through it and into the trees. He sought the place where the kid had crossed and found the fresh, light prints of the mustang. It was easy from that point. The three horsemen had been close enough to fire upon their prey, he noted. They had not done so.

In fact, if his ears served him well, the kid had fired the first shot. The gesture had been returned, but bullet holes in limbs far above the kid's head told him that the marksmen had not been serious. This gave him food for thought: Could it be that Duffy wanted the kid alive for some reason? If so, why?

He dismounted and trailed the reins and walked through dense brush among tall river oaks. The three men had retreated hastily under the fire he and Pit had laid down. This led him to believe that the attack had nothing to do with the cattle war, or with anything other than the capture of the kid on the mustang.

He went back and mounted the roan and rode down the riverbank. A mile or so toward the ranch house he found them. The kid had finished eating, the bag of vittles nearly empty, Pit was telling some story of the old days, and again all was peaceful in the land.

Sam stretched himself out on the grass and looked at the kid's white, oval face and big eyes. "Seems like you better stop hangin' around and settle down awhile."

"I'm okay. I take care of me." The voice was low and husky. "I keep tellin' you."

"They'd have run you down," Pit said. "That little pony's good, but its legs are short."

"I got my gun."

"You got a damn shotgun," said Sam. "You blasted at them, but you didn't hit anything."

"Kept 'em back till I could get past the bobwire."

"And then what?"

"I sorta figured you might be around." The big eyes stared back at him. "I just had a hunch."

Sam shook his head. "You were hangin' around earlier. I spotted your tracks comin' down the riverside. You knew we'd be hereabouts. Why'd you go back onto Duffy's land?"

"I got reason." For once, the kid seemed a bit confused.

"You want to be caught by Duffy?"

The fire flashed again in Mac's eyes. "Never in this world will he put a hand on me!"

"It don't figger," said Pit. "God knows we ain't got enough people to fight him. How in tarnation hell are you gonna do it all by your own self?"

"I'm still here."

"Why does Duffy want you so bad?" demanded Sam.

"Duffy's crazy." Now the kid was sullen. "How should I know?"

Sam said softly, "Kid, I got a notion you know damn

well. Best you should spit it out. Maybe it'll help everybody.''

The big eyes stared at him. Behind the kid, the river ran fast, overflowing from the previous rains. The sun beat down.

Pit said, ''And come stay at the ranch, blast ye. Act sensible.''

The mustang moved to the edge of the water, its muzzle lowered. The kid went to release the bit so that the animal could drink.

Sam said, ''It's right, you know. Sooner or later, they're going to corner you.''

The kid's head shook again; the chin remained stubborn. Suddenly, from the water, a huge river rat emerged, its buck teeth gleaming.

The kid uttered a small scream, leaping backward and releasing the bridle. A heel caught, and the kid was in the river, floundering, sputtering.

''Hell, he can't swim,'' said Sam. He ran and jumped into the river. Pit reacted identically, so that both of them were in the troubled waters, converging on the kid, reaching, grabbing, hauling. It was a clumsy operation, Sam thought, even as they dragged the slight form to the bank and deposited Mac on dry land, coat and vest open, the not-too-clean shirt clinging tightly against the kid's body.

Sam coughed water and then said, ''I'll be damned!''

Pit said, ''I jest don't flat believe it.''

As they stared, the kid ran, leaped up on the mustang, and was gone, back toward Duffy's precincts.

Sam said, ''Did you see what I saw?''

''Tits,'' said Pit. ''That's a damn girl!''

''That's a damn young woman,'' Sam said. ''Girls don't have tits like that.''

They stood, soaking wet, staring at each other. Then Sam sat down and began tugging at his boots. He said, ''I don't know about you, but I ain't ridin' back in wet duds.''

Pit said, ''Well, it ain't Saturday, but a bath never did hurt nobody, I reckon.''

They spread their garments on the dry grass. Pit squatted with a rifle at hand in case of trouble. Sam dove into the river.

The damn girl had slept in his room, he remembered now. He reassembled the lineaments of the kid in his mind's eye: the big dark eyes, the delicate chin, and the straight but shapely lips, the grace of movement. A young pretty woman emerged.

She had all the courage and know-how of a young man; and she was riding around, living off the land, toting a shotgun; fearless, self-contained far above average. It was impossible. But it was true.

Another woman rode a pinto pony across Duffy's land with impunity, crossed its border, and climbed into the hills. Frequenters of Duffy's Place would not have recognized Maizie. She wore buckskins. Her hair was braided long and dark upon her back. She wore no rouge or powder. There was no laudanum in her system.

She rode through alders and rock oak, and then through a canyon and followed an almost invisible trail. She was weary and bleary-eyed from lack of sleep, but she was palpitating with eagerness and anxiety. She came to the top of a small bluff on the bank of the Pecos River and drew in. She dismounted, tied the pinto, and unloaded a heavy saddlebag from which she extracted a small mirror. Her reflection showed lines at the corners of her eyes and running from her nostrils to the edges of her mouth. She shook her head, then found a spot of soft brush and lay down.

She could not let Soledad see her in this condition. She looked years older than she actually was. She was beaten down in spirit by the life she led, the life she had chosen rather than to marry another half-breed and become a drudge. She had no training, no skills. Duffy had been the sorrowful, sordid answer. Duffy and the blue liquid that was the solace and also the means of early death of the whores of the West.

One thing she had learned in order to stay alive—to relax. She lay perfectly still now, a small revolver at her side. She had lived a precarious existence, but she was not fearful; she was numbed. She had no future; she lived only in the present. Since she had met Soledad, it had been difficult, but she managed.

He was not a young boy, this son of a chief. He had children by his deceased wife. They had met on one of the rides Maizie took when material matters wore her down too far. The attraction was mutual, passionate—and doomed.

She had offered to go with him to his tribe and become his slave. He had refused because of the ignominy this would place upon her in the eyes of the other braves. Yet he could not give her up; thus they maintained these occasional special meetings whenever possible.

She slept. When she awoke, she shouldered the saddle-bag and took the path down the side of the bluff. At mid-point she fired the little revolver once, twice, paused, then fired again.

After a moment, there was an answering shot. Laboring under the heavy saddlebag, she made her way down to the end of the small ravine. Here the Comanches were seques-tered; here came tall Soledad, striding. Behind him the band lounged, indifferent, intent only on the beef they were broiling on a spit.

Soledad and Maizie embraced. Then they walked away, out of sight of the others. There were only a dozen of them all told, contrary to the belief of Duffy and others that a large band of Comanches were raiding. Soledad's tribe was far away on the high plain. He was here mainly because of Maizie—or Raven Santos, her real name.

She said, "I bring you gifts." They spoke the half Mexican, half Indian patois, not easily translated.

"I want only you," he told her.

"Look." She pulled boxes of cartridges from the saddlebag. "Bullets. From Duffy."

"Ah, Duffy."

"He wants you to raid the Crooked S. There are fine horses on that place. Duffy will help you, see that no harm comes to you. So he says."

"He says it out of both sides of his mouth." But Soledad accepted the ammunition. It was sorely needed. The settlers were too well armed, too alert in these times. "And what of you?"

"What can be for me?"

His arms went around her, but he had no comforting words. He led her to a grassy bank and they sat close together. He was not handsome; he was flat-nosed and scarred. He said, "The horses."

"Oh, yes. The horses." Comanches were nothing without good horses. They were Plains Indians, nomads, cavalry fighters.

"You will raid the Crooked S?" she asked.

"Not without more guns to go with the bullets. They watch at the Crooked S because of Duffy. Duffy must also provide us with guns."

She pulled away from him, her mouth hard. "So I must go back to Duffy and ask for guns."

"There are reasons why I cannot do what I wish."

"You will send me back to Duffy?"

"I do not want you to go back." He shook his head.

"You are the son of a chief. I am a woman, no longer a girl. Yet I am to get the bullets and the guns for you to steal horses and leave me."

"What can I say? My people are against you. Even the

young braves, my own men laugh behind my back. And my father sent a message.''

"Your father, the great chief," she said bitterly.

"It is time for the moon raid."

"Oh, yes. Time to raid into Mexico to steal horses and bring back slaves. And Mexican women."

"It is our way." He drew himself up. She had seen him like this before, withdrawn, stubborn.

"The mighty son of a great chief. Faithful to his tribe, unfaithful to his lover." The anger rose in her. "Raid into Mexico against people who cannot fight back. Like my father, Ramon Santos, who was brave enough to take one of your squaws and was killed by your people in the end."

"My people have suffered. The white-eyes have driven us here and there. . . ."

"You have no brains to make peace, to settle down. You love me, you say. You do nothing for me. You want guns? Take them from Duffy. I'll not bring them to you."

She got to her feet. He stood tall, staring at her. Words would not come to him.

She turned and ran. For a moment, it seemed he would follow. Then he folded his arms and stood, watching her go.

She ran all the way to the pinto pony, tears streaming. They were not the tears of a lovelorn girl, but tears of anger and frustration. She thought of Quanah Parker, leader of all Comanches and sometimes the Kiowa, their rival tribe, whose mother, Cynthia Ann, was a white woman captured by Comanches in 1836. Cynthia Ann had borne children to her chieftain husband and lived happily until "rescued" by the whites, and now, it was said, pined for her husband.

Quanah Parker was half white but accepted because his father had been an Indian. Had her father been a Comanche . . . She calmed herself. She was helpless. She thought of the solace of laudanum, the life in Duffy's Place where there were bright lights and laughter. Perhaps that was all there was in store for her. Soledad was lost, bound by tradition.

Maizie came to the cliff where she had left the pony. She realized that she was hungry. She had not shared the food with Soledad. She rode the pinto down a circuitous path to the river. She sat in the shade of an oak tree and munched. Her mind was clear. She had to decide whether to ask Duffy for the guns or to forget Soledad. She was accustomed to failure. Her life had been for nothing. She finished eating and stared at the river.

At last she got up as if mesmerized by the flowing water. She slowly divested herself of her clothing. She dove into the river and swam.

It would be easy to stop swimming and drift and let it all go, the miserable past, the black future.

She was at midstream when she heard his cry, and then she saw Soledad swimming toward her. She turned on her back and floated.

Bedraggled, clothing wrinkled and shrunken in parts, Sam and Pickens arrived at the ranch house barely before noon. As they changed in the bunkhouse, the old man said, "Been meanin' to go into town for supplies. Reckon I best do it today."

"I'll go," said Sam. "I got a notion or two to consider in Bowville."

"Stubby's so scared somethin' will go wrong with Mary, he won't leave. "

"Can't blame him." Sam pulled on his city clothing, thinking that he had better buy work garments for his stay on the Pecos, which might stretch longer than he had intended. He also had to learn what there was to know about the kid—the girl—who was running around loose, in daily danger. As for the range war, that was a matter of planning and acting in the right manner at the right time.

Above it all, he knew he had to inform Renee of what was going on. He sat on the edge of the bunk and oiled his revolver, taking great care.

Pickens said, "You're frettin' on that gal, ain't you?"

"Probably. How about you?"

"Sartain. Purely crazy, runnin' wild, playin' like a boy."

"And Duffy after her. Why?"

"She didn't say. Don't hardly have to wonder. Duffy's hell on women."

Sam added oil to the outer side of his gun belt and stretched it, working it in his hands. "There's got to be something we could do. Bring in the Rangers."

"You reckon? Maybe if you see the man . . . Keen, you said?"

"Maybe. What about the eatery fellow? Antonio."

"Good man in a tight spot. He's a friend of Stubby's," Pickens said.

"Uh-huh. I know." Sam frowned. "Just who is the local law in Bowville?"

"Ain't none since Howlin' Howley left a week or so ago. Some said he was paid off by Duffy."

"Howley from Dodge City? He got run out of there, years ago."

"He runs a lot," Pickens said. "Drunk too often for Duffy, they say. Forgot to take orders."

"Hard man, Duffy."

There was a horse and buggy in the yard when Sam went to the house. Indoors, Stubby walked the floor. Sam sat down and watched him, feeling as helpless as a hog on ice. It seemed a long while before a young, bearded man dressed in funereal black came downstairs. Stubby mumbled, "Dr. Conover . . . Sam Jones."

The young man said, "You must stop worrying, Mr. Stubbs. It is not helping your wife."

"Never mind me. How the hell is she?" demanded Stubby.

"The same." The young doctor appealed to Sam. "Can you make him understand that it is in the hands of nature? That Mrs. Stone is in no danger? That if she follows my directions and maintains rest and serenity, her chances of bearing a healthy child are good?"

Sam said, "Haven't had any experience in the matter. But if you say so, reckon Stubby better pay heed."

"She lost two, I told you. Dammit, one more and she'll pine away to nothin'," cried Stubby. "How can I not worry?"

"Just try not to show it." The doctor lowered his voice. "Tell her I have every reason to believe she'll be fine if she remains quiet, tranquil."

Sam said, "Sounds reasonable, Stubby. Put on an act. You were good at that some time back, remember?"

"You shut your mouth," said Stubby. He swallowed hard, then managed a weak grin. "See what you mean, Doc. You be back next week, you hear?"

"Of course. Please to meet you, Mr. Jones." Dr. Conover departed, stepping briskly like a man sure of himself.

Stubby said, "New boy. Old doc, he up and died. Mary misses him."

"This one can't do any worse," said Sam. "Seems like he knows what he's up to."

"Comes from some school back East. Harvard. Boston. He talks funny, you notice?"

"Talk don't do it. Now sit down, I got something to tell you." Sam proceeded to relate what had happened that morning.

Stubby's eyes were wide. "That kid's a gal? That ornery young maverick?"

"You can ask Pit. Damn good-lookin', too, when you consider everything."

"It don't make a lick o' sense." Stubby shook his head.

Then he asked, "Would you come upstairs and help me pretend?"

They went to Mary's room. She was sitting up, a smile on her face. She said, "He's nice, Dr. Conover. He says he's pretty sure it'll be a boy."

"How in tarnation—" Stubby brought himself up short. "Yep, he's a whole lot smarter than old Doc Steever. He says you're goin' to be fine, and I believe him."

"That's right," Sam said. "You want a boy, Mary?"

"I just want a baby, Sam," she said quietly.

She had put it all in that short sentence, he realized. It was new to him, but he could feel it in his heart. Never in his life had he felt the need of offspring, nor had he known anyone who did so. Now he absorbed it, wondering, not for the first time, how he could have lived so long and known so little about so many things. He said, "By the Lord Harry, you're goin' to make it, Mary. I'd bet my life on it."

As he went down the stairs soon after, it occurred to him that he might well be forced to bet his life on it.

Pickens had a pair of spanking bays hitched to a light wagon. He handed over a grimy piece of paper. "Can you read it?"

Sam said, "Just about."

"Better you shouldn't go huntin' that maverick kid. I know you. Best you should do what you got to do and get the hell back here where you might be needed."

"It'll be okay." Sam went into the bunkhouse and got his rifle and extra ammunition. It was not really good sense to be driving a team through Duffy country, or even into Bowville whence he might be forced to make a fast exit. As to the girl in boy's clothing, the record showed that he needn't hunt for her. She always seemed to appear in the vicinity.

He put the rifle on the seat, considered for a moment, then went back to his saddlebag and took out the twin of his Colt .44 and slid it beneath the blanket that served as a cushion on the seat of the wagon.

"Don't miss a bet, huh, Sam?" Pit Pickens grinned.

"Try not to." Sam went to the heads of the team and spoke to them, rubbing their noses. They were spirited, he saw, and built for speed.

Pickens said, "Harness-broke 'em myself. They'll do."

"Seems so. I'll be seein' you." Sam climbed into the wagon, picked up the reins, and clucked the team into action. They were well-gaited and willing. He drove toward town, turning over in his mind all that had happened since his arrival on the Pecos, the rifle beneath his knee, his eyes ever scanning the countryside.

At the Crooked S they were putting up a brave front, he knew. The odds against them were simply tremendous if Duffy made a strong move, if the Ranger did not interfere, if help could not be brought in. Probably Mary was acting much braver than she would let them know. No matter how he figured it, there was tragedy ahead.

He could kill Duffy.

That was something that still needed a lot of cogitation. Was it the right thing to do? The death of a rascal with no redeeming virtues that he could ascertain, was it correct to accomplish the deed?

He drove down the road through the land owned by Duffy. There was no sign of life, but once or twice he thought he was being observed. Would Duffy have him killed in cold blood?

There was no doubt about it. Duffy would do so in a minute if he could get away with it. Possibly only the presence of Ranger Keen prevented him from taking the chance. Didn't that give Sam Jones the right to challenge Duffy? He brooded as the bay team trotted along the road to Bowville.

And then there was the maverick kid. That was entirely beyond his experience. It was beyond reason, a girl roaming around alone, living off the land equipped with only a double-barreled shotgun and a mustang and a hell of a lot of nerve. Something had to be done—something like Pit Pickens's notion of Stubby taking her in.

A horseman came out of a copse of pine. Sam's rifle came to hand; he reined in.

Ranger Keen called, "You're mighty quick with that, Jones. I got complaints about you."

Sam pulled up the team, and Keen draped a leg over the horn of his saddle, grinning.

"Duffy cryin' on your shoulder?"

"Yep. Said you attacked his innocent cowboys."

"Do tell."

"Said a lot of things. They got a new marshal in town. Name of Simon."

"Well, now. That's a fearsome fella, that Simon."

Keen said, "Got a couple mean deputies, though."

"It figures."

"Tell me, you heard anything about Comanches around here?"

"Nary a word," said Sam.

"I got a telegram from headquarters. Brave called Soledad and some young 'uns. Comanches make everybody restless, even headquarters. I got to go and see."

"I'm the supply man," said Sam. "And the handyman. Just mindin' my business."

"And that of the Crooked S," said Keen. "It's a tight spot, Jones. I'll do what I can. Duffy cuts no ice with me."

"I appreciate it. So does Stubby."

"You're right to keep that rifle handy. I'll be doin' what I can. If I find the Comanches, I'll let you know. They'll be lookin' for horses at the least."

"Thanks," Sam said. "I'll pass the word."

Keen turned and rode into the trees. Sam continued on

the road. Now it was Indians, no less. The sun seemed unwilling to shine on the righteous these days, he mused.

He made it to Bowville without further incident. From the moment he entered the precincts of the town, he noted a change in atmosphere. It was as if a pall had been cast over all that moved. People walked in the late afternoon with quick steps, going about their business while looking over their shoulders. There were few kids on the street, only the tough boys who seemed subdued themselves. Even the dogs were wary.

Sam pulled up at the telegraph office. The clerk eyed him with unease. He considered a moment, then decided the less said the better. His message to Renee was: "Arrived okay. Letter follows." He hated to write, but he thought it safer and the hotel would have stationery.

He decided to put up the team and drove to the livery stable. The hostler looked at him with surprise, asking, "Ain't you from the Crooked S?"

"Yep."

"Well . . . all right. I'll take care of 'em."

"Any reason why not?" Sam asked.

"Just that things are . . . different lately."

"I see. Keep 'em handy for hitchin', you hear?"

"That's what I mean. Things are . . . different."

"I heard you the first time." Sam paid in advance and walked back from the edge of town toward Antonio's eatery. He remembered that he had left his spare gun on the seat of the wagon, then decided to take a chance on that. He continued on through the town, meeting people who, unlike normal Texans, evaded his glance. Although it was nearly suppertime, the restaurant was empty of customers. The stout owner came out slowly from the kitchen. His face lit up.

"Hey, it's sure good to see you, Sam Jones. This place is a damn morgue unless Duffy gives his okay. There's all hell to pay around here."

"I noticed," Sam said. "Got yourself a new lawman and all that."

"Uh-huh. The sumbitch." Antonio produced a flat bottle from under his apron. "You look like a man needs a drink." He poured generously into two tumblers on the table at the window. Sam put his hat on the floor and sat down.

"I hear Duffy's bringin' in more ranch hands." Antonio went on. "Gunners, you can bet. The Ranger ain't been around. You think Duffy might be goin' too damn far?"

"Depends," said Sam. "Fella like him, he makes a move, grabs what he can, then puts the blame on other people. Then he's got it and it's hard to take it away from him."

Across the street, the doors of Duffy's Place swung open. A man in a checkered suit and derby hat came flying out, rolled down steps and into the street. Simon and the two guns, Jackson and Magrew, followed leisurely, picked up the victim, and shook him. Playing cards and a few coins scattered. The three then converged and took their prisoner away.

Antonio said, "Gamblin' man named Checkers Moseby. He's been winnin' pretty good this week. Seems honest enough, but you know Duffy."

"I don't know as much about Duffy as I'd like to know. Seems you do come by a heap of information somehow or other."

"Funny thing. Maizie, that dark gal, one of Duffy's two favorite whores, she gets high on laudanum and yammers to me sometimes. You saw her when you were here last. It's like she trusts me."

"You're a trustworthy man," said Sam. "She tell you anything important?"

"Sometimes she goes on about her Injun friend. Sometimes she says how she wants to get outa here. She sure hates Duffy."

"Interestin'," said Sam. "You still got food?"

"Sure, I got plenty. Duffy, he comes in here because I got good food. But nobody else but him and his."

"How long can you stay in business thataway?"

"Until Duffy takes me over. Like he's takin' over the whole town."

Sam said, "If you can spare me another shot of that good stuff and bring me what I had before, I'll ponder on it."

"You got enough trouble with the Crooked S," Antonio told him. He poured the drink and then went back to the kitchen. Now he seemed to be doing the cooking himself. That was Duffy again, influencing the life of an honest, hard-working citizen.

Maizie was the dark whore he remembered from his first encounter with Duffy. Another woman in the case; his life was becoming complicated with them. It wasn't particularly different at that, he admitted. Mainly he had been a man of the towns with no desire for hunting or fishing or lonely treks into the wilderness. He drank the whiskey and relaxed. It had been a long day.

Antonio came with the food at last. Sam ate, watching Duffy's Place while the restaurant man prattled nervously on and on. "I'd close up and go on out with you and join Stubby, but they're watchin' me close. Watchin' everybody."

Men went in and out of Duffy's Place. Evidently it was the only joint in town, now, and Texans would have their gambling, whiskey, and women. Sam finished the meal.

"Good grub," he told Antonio. "And now look, we got company."

Simon slid into the restaurant, a sawed-off shotgun in his hands. He said in his loud, arrogant voice, "Sam Jones, you're under arrest."

From behind Antonio, the gunner added, "I wouldn't try anything, Jones."

If he did make a move, Sam thought, Antonio would surely be caught in the crossfire. And if they got him, there would still be Duffy in charge, dead marshals or no dead marshals. He put his gun on the table and asked, as if it mattered, "What are the charges?"

Now Duffy entered, Maizie and the other whore on his arms. He affected surprise. "Now what can be goin' on here? This is amazin'."

Simon recited, "We're arrestin' Cemetery Jones on charges of assault with intent to kill."

"Oho! He did try to kill some of our poor cowboys, now, did he not?"

"Beg to differ," said Sam. "If I'd have wanted to kill them, they'd be dead. They were trespassin', you see. Just warned them off." His mind was working with its usual speed. They evidently did not dare to kill him outright for fear of Ranger Keen. It would be best to play for time.

Simon said, "There, y'see? A dangerous criminal. You'll just walk out the door and down the street, Jones."

"You'll have a lawyer. I'll see to it meself," said Duffy sympathetically. "After all, you did not hit any of the lads. Justice must be done."

"And you got witnesses to vow that you said that." Sam picked up his hat, got up from the table. "Very neat, Duffy."

"Ah, well, a man like you, so well known. You've got friends to come to your rescue," said Duffy. "Just trot along to the hoosegow, now, and we'll see what we shall see when the circuit judge comes to Bowville."

"In another month or so?"

"Six weeks, I believe." Duffy was smiling. "You'll be fed and cared for, I expect. This town ain't the tulies. This is a good town."

"You're a brave man, Duffy," said Sam. "You can stand there and talk and almost believe what you're sayin'."

"Git goin'," Jackson, the gunner, said behind him. "Palaver ain't helpin' nothin'."

Sam obeyed. He caught a glance from Maizie that puzzled him, half sympathetic, half dull acceptance of defeat. The other girl was giggling and wiggling against Duffy; Maizie stood apart. Something was there, but it was not the time for him to make an exploration, that was for sure.

He said, "One moment, please. I owe the gentleman for a meal." He was very careful reaching into his pocket. Simon snatched his gun from the tabletop. "No sweat." He produced a gold coin and dropped it on the table. "Thanks for everything," he said to Antonio.

He could have beaten Simon to the revolver. He could have downed Duffy before they got him. He knew all that even as he rejected the notion.

Simon said, "March right on into the street, Jones."

Sam walked before the other two, Simon at his side. The gunmen knew better than to get within arm's reach of him. Simon knew nothing, swaggering pigeon-breasted toward the jail, which was at the end of town next to the livery stable, a fact Sam had noticed long before when he was conning the terrain.

People stared, but no one commented. The day had diminished to half-dusk.

Simon had a large key. It was an old jail, complete with an office for the marshal, and in a sad state of dirty confusion. There was one large, iron-barred cell. Jackson and Magrew watched silently as Simon opened the door and Sam walked in, then heard the slap of the big key in the lock.

Jackson said, "That won't hold him 'ceptin' you set and keep your eye open."

"What the hell you think I'm gonna do?" Simon looked curiously at the butt of Sam's revolver, then put it in the drawer of an old, sagging desk. "Send some kid over to clean up this joint, you hear? It's a damn mess."

"I'll tell the boss about it."

"And one of you's got to spell me."

"I'll see what the boss says."

From behind the bars, Sam observed, "You brave boys allowed to take a leak without askin' the boss?"

The two gunmen surveyed him with cold eyes. "If it wasn't for the boss, you'd be deader'n a mackerel."

"Could be," said Sam. "On t'other hand . . ." He smiled at them. A hanging kerosene lamp gave a flickering light. He felt the danger in the pair of them, the blond man and the dark one. They did not fear him. They acted out the drama as they were ordered by the man who paid them, without fear or conscience. These were not cowboys gone wrong, these were men born to be predators. Where they were from and how they got here was something of which only they were aware. They were a breed apart and Sam knew all about them. He watched them depart, then saw Simon sit down at the desk and burrow among papers left in disorder. Sam turned back into the cell.

There were four bunks, cracked and filthy, one atop the other on opposite walls. There was a high, open, barred window through which not even a midget could crawl. There was a waste can, battered and stinking. And there was a figure curled up on the lower bunk on the south wall.

The figure moved and a slightly cracked but smooth voice said, "Lamar V. Moseby here, sir. I take it you are known colloquially as Cemetery Jones."

"Right, but how'd you know?" Sam went closer and recognized the slight man in the checkered suit.

"Heard some confabulations amongst the philistines." He sat up, a slight man with slightly dulled handsome features. He had been badly mauled but seemed to be in one piece. He shook himself. "No bones broken at any rate. They did toss me about some." His speech was soft and slow, and the words seemed chosen with care. "Odd, y'know. I was not cheatin'. Merely winning."

"Winnin's all right in some places. Others, it's an invitation to big trouble."

"So I've noticed." Moseby squinted at him. "It appears that you, sir, are in high danger."

"You might say so."

"This fella Duffy, he has large plans. Empire-minded, from what I could gather."

"You gather real good." The man was educated, and there was something likeable in him.

"Seems a bit far-fetched, doesn't it?" Moseby observed.

"Seems so."

"Fella named Jeff Davis and some others tried it. Neighbors of mine, suh. I come from Alabama."

"That figures," said Sam. "Old Jeff and them, they put up a pretty good fight, I hear. Wasn't in it myself."

"Nor I. A losin' fight is not a good fight. Look at the two of us."

"We're alive," Sam said.

"Ah, yes." Moseby smiled.

Sam examined the walls of the cell. They had been well built with native stones years ago. The window was out of the question. He sat down on the bunk opposite his cellmate.

Moseby said, "I notice they didn't search you. They took everything from me, stake money, everything."

"They can wait. They mean to kill me, you see."

"Ah." Moseby paused, then said in a whisper, "Then it is imperative that we escape from here."

"Imperative is a good word. Trouble is, they built this joint too good." Sam paused. "Further and more, they would like nothin' better than to have me break out."

"They would be lying in wait to shoot you."

"If there wasn't a Texas Ranger around, they would have already done so."

"Not a cheerful prospect. They would not choose to leave a witness, now, would they, suh?"

"Probably not."

"Ah. Then we are in the hands of the lady."

"Lady?"

Moseby said, "The blindfolded lady who holds in her hand the scales of justice."

"I've seen her on a couple of courthouses," Sam said. "You count on her?"

"Despite all evidence to the contrary. If I had been cheating, you see, I would not hold the faith. If you were the bad man they claim you are, I would not believe in you."

Sam scratched his head. "A lady, huh?" A big rat ran across the floor, pursued by one even bigger. He thought of the kid and how nothing scared her except the river rat. He said, "I won't go against ladies nohow. But this is a hell of a place to look for one."

He thought of Renee up in Sunrise who had received his telegram by now and would be awaiting the promised letter. He thought of Mary Stone awaiting her baby. It did not improve his spirits to think of these ladies.

The soft voice went on. "Back home I have a mother and two lovely sisters, impoverished, like so many, by the War Between the States. They depend largely upon me for their sustenance. They are very proper people, you see; they believe I am a prospector. For gold. Humorous, isn't it?"

"Not particl'ry. Gold is where you find it." The southerner was a nice man, Sam thought, possibly a very clever fellow. It seemed a deep shame that he should be trapped in this dire situation.

"Exactly. And life is what you make of it. And all that. So much has been written, so much said. An ending in this squalid place is too shameful to contemplate."

"It is, at that." Sam made another round of the cell,

probing the walls, estimating the size of the window. It was hopeless.

He was beneath the high window when he heard a familiar voice. Hardly above a whisper, it said, "Sam? You there?"

"I'm here."

"I'm standin' on the saddle. Talk fast."

Sam said, "I got a gun beneath the blanket on Stubby's wagon. I could use two."

The voice of the maverick kid said, "I'll be back."

Moseby asked softly, "Now who was that?"

"A lady," said Sam. "You sure call the shots, friend."

5

Duffy sat in the private room behind the saloon, arrayed in all his glory: Mexican sash around his ample middle, high, soft, black boots, embroidered jacket. He held a glass of whiskey in his hand. The blond girl knelt at his side, ready with a bottle. Maizie sat on a stool nearby. The light-haired Jackson leaned against the wall.

Duffy said, "Cemetery Jones. Not human, is he? Got him where I want him, have I not? The dumb bastard, comin' into town alone."

"They can't find the Ranger, boss," Jackson reminded him. "We need the Ranger to pull it off."

Duffy exploded, "Sufferin' cats and dogs, we can't find the damn kid, we can't find the Ranger, what the hell can we do, and me payin' a fortune for help?" He jumped up and strode back and forth. He stopped in front of Maizie and snapped, "Guns. Your goddamn pulin' Injuns must have guns, is it now?"

"The bullets are no good without guns," she said.

He swung an arm. The back of his hand knocked her from the stool. "Tellin' me my business now, are ye? Stayin' away from the blue stuff, a big lady y'are, now. Guns!"

Jackson said in his expressionless voice, "Ranger seems to be lookin' for the Comanches, near as we can tell. Mebbe you better stop knockin' Maizie around and send her up there with some guns and orders to stay clear of Keen. Ranger gets killed, the whole damn battalion's on our asses."

"Don't you think I know that?" Duffy swallowed whiskey, choked, sputtered.

"Uh-huh. So you want it to look like Jones kills the Ranger. It ain't all that easy."

"We've got Jones's gun. We put the Ranger by the jail and let Jones out, and that's it."

"If we kill the Ranger nice and clean, no witnesses." Jackson shrugged. "Neat whizzer. If it works."

"It will work, damn your eyes."

Jackson's drawl did not alter. "If I'm to be damned, Duffy, which ain't no bad bet, it won't be by you. Me and Magrew is the ones you need. Simon's a fartin' fool."

"Simon can take his chances at the shootout when the Ranger gets to the jail. I want that Ranger. And I want that damn kid. And nobody's doin' whatso-damn-ever about them."

"You want me to start lookin'?"

Duffy hesitated. He looked long at the two guns tied down low on the lean flanks. He shook himself. "No, goddammit. I want you to get somebody to help, somebody with the brains God gave a goat."

Jackson said, "Okay. About the guns for the Injuns . . . ."

"Yes. Dig up a few. Maizie, you take 'em to wherever the hell your whorin' Injun's skulkin'."

She nodded, keeping her face turned so that he would not see the scarlet mark left by his blow nor the hatred in her eyes she knew she could not control. Jackson strolled to the rear door and she followed him into the night.

The gunslinger said, "Might tell you, I ain't for slappin' women around."

"Thanks. That helps a lot," she snarled.

"Man pays wages. I'm for hire. I can manage some decent Winchesters for your friend Soledad. You can get a pack pony at the livery stable. I'll handle all o' that."

A few paces farther on she asked, "Tell me, why do you work for Duffy? Seems to me you got more common sense and brains than him."

He looked away from her, off into the distance. "The way things rattle, Maizie. Once I was a boss wrangler. Man said somethin' about my mom."

"And you killed him."

"My mom was a whore. But it wasn't right for him to say it, now was it?"

"I been a whore."

"You see what I mean, then."

"Ain't anybody to take up for me," Maizie said.

"Not your Injun?"

"Not the way it is. Like you say, it's the way things rattle."

"But you'll take him the guns."

"I got to do what seems best. God knows I ain't able to rightly tell what's best, but I got to do it. Whatever." She was on the verge of tears.

Jackson said, "I don't know anything whatsoever about women. But seems like what you're askin' me goes both ways. Why are *you* workin' for Duffy?"

"Damned if I truly know."

"The way things rattle," he said.

It wasn't good enough, but she had no words to express her feelings at the moment. They were approaching the dark end of town where the fringe people dwelt, where no one asked questions, where a cantina run by a Mexican was the focal point of all action.

She asked, "This fella Jones. Who is he, anyway?"

"Cemetery Jones? Hell, he's the best gun in the country," said Jackson.

"Where's he from?"

"Damn if I know. Lives up in Sunrise. Sorta owns the town, they say."

"Why is Duffy so scared of him?"

"Well, Jones is a friend of Stubby's. And Duffy wants the Crooked S."

"So you just plain murder Jones."

"That's the way it rattles."

"Like the snake. Only without warnin'." She shook her head. "And now I'm takin' guns to Soledad and he'll try to kill Stone, and everything will turn out for Duffy. What about us? You and me and Magrew and all?"

"I dunno about you, but I'll move on. There'll be more Rangers around, and me and them don't get along."

"And where would I go?"

He said kindly, "Maizie, where do all whores go? You marry some jasper or you take too much laudanum. This country's damn hard on women and dogs."

. They went into the cantina and Jackson spoke to the owner, then they went out back, where there was a cow shed, which stank, and beneath a heap of manure were rifles wrapped in canvas. Jackson handed over money and then the rifles were stacked with precision on a small horse, which was surprisingly docile.

Jackson said, "You go change your duds and I'll bring it along. I wish you luck with Soledad."

Maizie said, "Luck ain't what it is. Just the way things rattle."

She hurried through the dark back alleys to Duffy's Place and up to the cubicle allowed to her. She changed into the worn buckskins. There was a half-empty bottle of the blue liquid on her small table. She picked it up, opened it, then put it down again. It was no longer a solace to her, she suddenly realized. It was a temporary escape, but there was Soledad, and there were the guns and what must be done. There were no alternatives; she was on her own and only time would tell her story.

As she was putting the laudanum bottle down and picking up her Smith & Wesson .32 revolver, the door crashed open and Duffy stalked into the room. "Ah, me little mavourneen," he said. "I see you're on your way to the bloody Comanche."

"Jackson got the guns."

"He did, he did. And the Injuns will come down on the Crooked S and we'll be right behind 'em, you see, lass? And then all will be well." He reached out to embrace her and the fumes of whiskey stopped her breathing for a moment. Then she slipped away from him. With the revolver in her hand, she was a hairsbreadth close to killing him.

She did not pull the trigger. She knew she would never get out of town alive if she followed her instinct. She drew a deep breath and then said, "I'll be off."

He roared, "Just a minute there, me beauty—"

But she was gone down the backstairs and into the night, and Jackson was there with her pony and the pack animal and a wave of the hand as she rode off to the hills.

Duffy went down the stairway to the saloon. Business was slack; it had been growing less of late. Texans shied away from monopolies, but they came here because it was the only game in town. He had to be cautious, he thought, signaling to the bartender and roaring, "Drinks are on the house. Belly up, my friends. Good times are a-comin'."

Jackson came in the back way and nodded to him. They went into the office. Duffy said, "Now, m'boy, we're all set, y'see? Just get that Ranger in here and all will be fine and dandy. Keep a watch."

"Magrew and two others are outside, Simon's inside."

"But no word of the Ranger?"

"Maizie's gone to the Comanches; mebbe the Ranger'll

follow her. Then when he knows where the Injuns are, he'll be around, mebbe to send one of his telegrams.''

"Get him before he sends it."

"That's the thing to do, all right."

"The Rangers will be welcome as springtime if we can make it seem Jones killed this one. Ah, it's a fine scheme," Duffy said.

"You need me anymore tonight?"

"Best to see that the boys are in the right places. I depend on you, Jackson. You've got more savvy than the others."

Jackson nodded and went out into the street. Instead of going to the jail, he slipped into the other bar, the one in the hotel. He was weary of it, all the plotting and planning. His guns seemed heavy on his thighs. He untied the holsters, ordered a double whiskey, and relaxed.

In the quiet town of Sunrise, Renee Hart ran her fingers over the keys of the piano. Marshal Donkey Donovan stood by nursing a beer. The night was pleasant; the customers in El Sol were enjoying themselves.

Donkey said, "Not to worry, Miss Renee. Sam's always taken care."

"I know." She smiled at him, but the music did not rise above the note of dolor, music neither Donkey nor any other present could identify but which always pleased them. They did not know Wagner from Beethoven, but they knew Renee's artistry by instinct.

"The telegram didn't say anything bad."

"I know," she replied. She could not explain well that between them she and Sam had an empathy born of their mutual love, something even she did not quite understand and of which Sam had only a confused notion.

"Mebbe I should take a leave and go down there," Donkey said.

She looked up at him. "If Sam is in danger, no one man

can help. Sam's worth a dozen, isn't he? Your job is here."

"It's real quiet here."

"The lull before the storm," she told him, cascading notes with a heavy left hand. "Just keep hoping the odds are not too great on the Pecos."

Donkey nodded. "Yes'm. You're right. You're always right, somehow or t'other."

She broke into "Buffalo Gals Won't You Come Out Tonight," and at the poker table Mayor Wagner sang lustily in a natural, fine baritone and others joined in until the rafters rang and the dance-hall girls got up and whirled around in their full dresses. Renee had no wish to convey her inner disturbance to the multitude.

Stubby Stone sat at the end of the long kitchen table with a mug of coffee and said, "Damn fool thing, Sam goin' into town alone."

Pit Pickens shook his gray head. "You aim to stop Sam when he's a mind to do somethin'?"

"He was always sudden. You know, Pit, long as I've knowed him, I've got no idea where he comes from? Who was his family? He was a loner, always a loner."

"He's seen the elephant. This country, no man's got to lay out a map of hisself."

Stubby mused. "I remember the shootout. There was three of 'em, y'know. Two in front, one in back. They come on fast. Sam had that gun of his'n out before you could say spit. He got the first one in the head. You ain't supposed to head-shoot, but it took the jasper out, y'see? He gut-shot the second."

"And you got numero trey."

"I thought I was somewhat fast. Sam had the first one down before I drawed."

"He's got the hands."

"There's somethin' different about Sam. I dunno. I

dealt him a dirty deal I was so crazy mad about Mary. He never said diddley doo to me or anybody. He just rode out."

Pit lit a corncob pipe and blew foul smoke. "Been around a long time, Stubby. Seen a lot. People is critters. One bad thing don't make a good man rotten. You never crossed nobody since that time. You and Mary are fine together. Sam, he's another animule."

"He say anything to you 'bout what he does in that town, that Sunrise?"

"On'y that it's peaceable and that he's got a stake. Had to ask him. People talk to old men more."

"You ain't never goin' to be old." Stubby finished his coffee. "Better make sure Mary's sleepin' good."

"I'll be moseyin' around. Don't need so much sleep anymore. Got to see the boys is watchin'."

"Couldn't do without you, Pit."

Stubby went upstairs. Pickens sat for a moment, thinking of his own life, his dead wife, a boy he hadn't seen in long years. He thought of his time with Stubby and he thought of Sam Jones. It had been a damn fool thing to drive a wagon into Bowville. But Sam, now, he was a different kind of man. Best to let him do things his own way. And there was that loco, little maverick gal; what of her? Life didn't get any less interesting with old age, he decided with a grin.

In the dim reflected light from the lamp in the office of the jail, Sam listened to the soft cadence of Checkers Moseby's voice. "You would think that a gamblin' man would be quick with a pistol. Most of us wear a shoulder holster as you well know, suh. But early on I noted that men carrying short guns often got themselves eradicated in some foolishness, most often drunken. It also came to my attention that in the West unarmed men are seldom shot at."

"Never thought of it that way," said Sam. "True."

"You give a red-blooded young man a revolver to hang on his hip and a few shots of redeye and somethin' is bound to explode. Sooner or later."

"It happens," Sam admitted. It had happened to him, much to his annoyance and sometimes to his sorrow.

"A rifle, now, suh, is a thing of beauty. A rifle is for shootin' birds and beasts, for food or sport. I must say, I pride myself on my ability with a rifle."

"That's just fine. If we had one." Sam's mind was on the maverick kid—the female maverick kid. Long gun, short gun, there was a time and a place for everything. He would be no good to Stubby or Mary or anyone else if one or the other was not provided soon. "Thing is, podner, if we get out of here alive, it'll be with a six-gun."

"Ah! You have me. But, suh, you are not responsible for me, now, are you?"

"You might not think so. Howsomeever, if we do make it, there's need for a rifleman to go against Mr. Duffy."

"You don't say? Is it the range war of which I have heard some talk?" Checkers asked.

"It is. Friend of mine owns the Crooked S."

"Cattle. Ugh. I am, suh, a city fella. I ride, of course. All south'ners ride. But cows?"

Sam observed dryly, "Cattle. Longhorns. Different sorta animals. They run a lot. Then you eat 'em, after they're fattened somewhat."

"Of course. My error, Mr. Jones. Sounds somewhat like a skirmish is on its way."

"And then some. Can you shoot from the saddle?" Sam asked.

"I can't say, suh, never havin' tried. Could be."

"Then you better ride drag with me."

"Drag, suh?"

"Just follow along best you can. If the time comes."

Time had been getting away. There was another man,

wearing two guns tied low, in the office with Simon now, a mean-looking, low-browed fellow. Simon was gesturing, posturing. His loud voice came faintly as Sam motioned for silence and listened. He heard: "That damn Ranger . . . Sure. . . . We got Jones's gun. . . . You leave it to Duffy. . . ."

At the high window came a sibilant whistle. Jones crawled up, Checkers giving him a hand. The revolver came through between the narrow-set bars and the familiar voice said, "Gotta run. They're patrolin'."

"Missy Mac, or whoever, you get yourself out to the Crooked S, you hear me?" Sam shot at her. "There's goin' to be a whizbang and I want you out of it."

"Don't you call me 'missy.' You take care of you." She was gone.

"Dammit to hell," said Sam, coming down to the floor of the cell. The rats ran again, for the twentieth time, chasing each other. "Okay, Mr. Moseby. Just be ready."

"Drag, suh. I'm ridin' drag," said Checkers coolly.

"Not right now. You're havin' a conniption fit."

"I beg your pardon?"

"Like fallin' down and hollerin'. A screamin' meemies fit."

"Oh!" Moseby howled. He threw himself on the floor and writhed and squirmed and moaned.

Sam called, as politely as possible, "Marshal, this man needs attention."

Simon came around the partition that separated the office from the cell. He peered. Moseby yelped.

Sam presented his revolver. He said in a low voice, "If you want to live, Mr. Marshal, send your friend there for a doctor."

Simon turned fish-belly white, staring into the barrel of the revolver. He said, "Uh, Max, you better get the doc. The man's goin' loco here."

The man said, "What the hell do you care? The hell with the bastid."

For a moment, there was nothing in the air but static. Then Sam grasped Simon by his belt and yanked him up against the cell bars. He called, "You, Max, you want to live?"

The gunman's hand shot down. Sam fired past Simon's ear. The man called Max fell down with his gun half-drawn.

Sam said, "You see, Marshal, I just about saved your life. He would've got you before he got me. So be a nice fella and unlock this cage."

Simon gasped. "I don't . . . I can't . . ."

"You don't want to die right now, do you?" Sam's voice became very cold. "I just killed one man. I ain't anxious to add another."

Simon said, "Omigod! The keys. My belt." He was choking and sweating with animal fear.

Sam said, "Checkers, you got free hands, you do the honors."

Moseby was deft, extricating the keys, unlocking the cell door. Sam prodded Simon into the shabby office. There was a single window with a slightly torn shade. "Pull it down, Marshal, we need a bit of privacy," Sam said.

Simon obeyed, his hands shaking. His eyes shifted often to the dead man on the floor. Moseby spotted the customary cabinet of rifles on one wall, ran for it, extracted a Remington, and filled his pocket with shells from a convenient pasteboard box.

Sam said, "Take a look in the desk. There's a gun of mine around here someplace." He pushed the revolver against the bulge around Simon's middle. "You said somethin' about the Ranger? Like he might be done away with? Maybe with my gun? That wasn't too smart. Might've worked, though."

Moseby said, "I expect this is yours." He handed over Sam's gun. "And looky here. Money. My stake, no doubt."

"No doubt," Sam said. He addressed himself to Simon, who seemed unable to refrain from looking at the dead man. "Now it seems we got a bit of picklement here. If I walk you out, they might just as well shoot you and then shoot us, that patrol Duffy's workin'."

"They will. They will," Simon whispered. "It wouldn't work for you."

"So we got to wait here a bit."

There could be a lot of bloodshed, Sam thought. What with his two short guns and the gambler's rifle, it would be a small war. It could not be won, and Duffy would certainly not permit himself to be in range. Duffy paid others to take that risk.

"I'll do whatever you say," Simon pleaded. "But they'll kill me for sure."

"Now that would be a shame," said Sam. "I got a fast team and a wagon right next door. There's got to be some way for two men to manage this here whizzer."

"I can harness a team," proffered Moseby.

"If they'd let you." Sam shook his head. "You and me, we got responsibilities. Your family back home. My friends . . . No, it's got to be some kinda miracle."

"Miracle? Mr. Jones, suh, I purely cannot believe in miracles. Uncommon sense, yessuh."

Sam looked at the dead man. "If his clothes fit, I could make a break. But there's two jaspers out there, Jackson and Magrew, and they got eyes."

"I noticed the gentlemen," said Moseby. "Bad news."

"Sometimes a hat." He picked up the man's hat. It came down over his ears. He replaced his Stetson. "No, it's got to be one or t'other. Uncommon sense, like you say. Or a miracle."

Outdoors there was an explosion. Sam went to the

window, looked carefully through a crack in the shade. People were running.

The most feared cry of all Western towns rent the sky.

"Fire!"

He said, "The hell with how it happened. That's it!"

He shoved Simon into the cell and locked it. He came back to the window and watched. They were running toward Duffy's Place. He said to Checkers, "It's uncommon sense, I'll bet my life. And yours, podner."

Not a soul took notice as they walked in shadows to the livery stable. With both of them working quickly, it was only a matter of moments before the bays were hitched.

Sam said, "Came here to do an errand. Might's well get it over with."

He drove around to the rear of the general store. The owner, working over his accounts, saw him, and let him in. Sam said, "Got a list here. We can help. Here's money for it."

The gambler said, "You are a strange man, suh. Real thorough in your way."

When they swung back onto the street, they could see Duffy swinging his arms, shouting orders. It did not seem to be much of a fire. There were no red flames dancing against the night sky. There was a crowd, and he saw Duffy's men keeping it under control, and he could hear the noise.

He turned the team onto the road for the Crooked S. The mustang came flying past him. He shouted, "You little female devil, you get on to Stubby's house, you hear me?"

There was no sign that she heard. She rode the mustang straight ahead into the darkness. Sam swore some.

Moseby said, "So that's the 'uncommon sense.' "

"You could say that," Sam told him. "You could also opine that she started the fire."

He drove the bays at a spanking pace, although he did not feel there would be pursuit. He still half believed in miracles. Otherwise how come the maverick kid was always around at the exact right time?

Or was she indeed possessed of uncommon good sense?

The fire was easily put out. The crowd dwindled. Duffy was blowing hard; no one was listening. Jackson was very quiet, full of whiskey.

Duffy raved. "Coal oil. Smell the damn stuff. Someone made a pile o' rubbish and set it on fire."

A clerk from the general store ventured, "Somebody stole a can of coal oil when I wasn't lookin' earlier this evenin'."

"Nobody's lookin' anytime, anywhere," howled Duffy.

A boy among those who had flocked, as always, to the fire said, "I saw that kid on the mustang foolin' around. Darn kid hit me not long ago. Mean bastid."

"The kid?" Duffy frothed at the corners of his mouth. "The kid was in town and nobody— Damn my eyes to hell, where was everybody alla time?"

Jackson, who felt his several strong drinks, observed, "You had 'em watchin' the jail."

"By God, we'll just go down to the jail and see what happened to Simon," said Duffy. "He could've come to help put out my fire."

"Might be he thought he ought to watch the prisoners," Jackson said.

"I want to see that goddamn Cemetery Jones in a cell. If he . . ." Duffy paused. Then he took Jackson to one side. "Supposin' he got out? Supposin', everyone agreein', he set the fire? He could be hanged for that."

Jackson said, "You want to run that whizzer, boss, you better have a damn good story for Keen. Nobody's seen the Ranger."

"To hell with the Ranger." Duffy was beside himself with rage and frustration. "Let's get down to the jail."

They went to the jail, Jackson, Duffy, and the silent Magrew. They opened the door and stopped in their tracks at the sight of the dead man on the floor.

"Cemetery Jones," murmured Jackson. "They sure named him good."

"Where the hell is Simon?" demanded Duffy.

"I'm here," came a weak voice. "Jones somehow got a gun on us."

"Holy jumpin' Moses on a wheel," howled Duffy. "He even took the goddamn cardsharp with him."

"Does things up brown," said Jackson.

"Where's the damn keys?"

Simon said mournfully, "They took the keys with 'em."

"Real damn thorough," repeated Jackson.

"Well, get the blacksmith. Clean up this mess. Bury that damn Max. Keep your mouths shut about all of this," Duffy said. "Things have come to a pretty pass. It's time to move, m'boys. Time to get into somethin' we know we can win."

"Yep," said Jackson. "Sure is, before we all go the way of poor old Max there."

"Get 'em together. You ramrod it, m'boy. And that kid. Put some goddamn tracker on that kid."

"Whatever you say, boss." Jackson frowned, the whiskey in him working. "Would that mean more dinero?"

"Do the job, and you'll get more than you can believe, Jackson. More than you can believe."

Jackson thought, A bullet in the back? Not if I watch the phony Irishman. Not if Magrew and me watch him. Still, the job was there and it was a big deal. The biggest, he told himself.

The moon shone on the bluff above the Pecos, a coyote sang his mournful song, and the river ran strong and relentless when Maizie pulled up. Soledad awaited her; still, she made a small camp with her pinto and the pack animal. She was clumsy attending the animals, but she needed time.

It was strange how abstinence from the drug of the whores altered her feelings. She had never been stupid. She had behaved as she believed she must in order to survive—barely survive. She had believed in Soledad, that somehow he would rescue her as in the tales told among the girls in the casinos. Every whore believed that a man would come along to take her to his ranch and make her pregnant and give her a life to live. The more laudanum they took, she knew, the more they believed it.

They thought she was lucky, the girls in Duffy's Place. They thought she was favored by the boss. She had been in El Paso, in Pecos; she had met Soledad while in Pecos and when she had come to Bowville, it was because he had refused to take her away to the tribe. And now what was she?

A messenger of ill will, bearing arms to her lover so that he could return in glory to Quanah Parker and kill Mexicans and take slaves. In the meantime, he was to help kill Stubby Stone and Cemetery Jones and most likely the lady who was going to have the baby; possibly the killer would not be Soledad himself but one of his braves who would kill anything white-skinned that came within reach.

Was she a white woman in her heart? Why did she pause before carrying out her mission? She made a small fire, not to heat the food she carried but to frighten away the spirits that were affecting her clear mind, a mind free of laudanum and promises unkept.

She sat cross-legged in her buckskins, the Smith & Wesson .32 at hand. She was not truly afraid of living things, it was her thoughts that caused her to shiver.

A husky voice said, "Just put that gun down, Maizie."

She was so startled that she dropped the revolver into the little fire. A small figure came up like the ghosts she feared and snatched it away.

"Waste not, want not," said the voice. The maverick kid put the gun in the pocket of a dilapidated coat and sank down on the opposite side of the fire, shotgun across the knees. "Let's you and me talk."

"I . . . Who the hell are you?"

"Just Mac. Call me Mac."

"You're the kid Duffy's after," Maizie said.

"You could put that both ways. . . ."

"You're scary, you know that? Just a kid, but you scare people."

"That's part of it. Now, about those guns you're totin'. Are they for the Comanches?"

"How the hell do you know— None of your business."

"Oh, I know a heap. I make it my business to know just about all that goes on around Bowville. Nobody pays much attention to a kid."

Maizie said, "Some kid." Her fear was mysteriously fading. She was curious now. "Why does Duffy want you so bad?"

"That's my business. Why are you carrying guns to the Indians?"

"That's my business."

"No. That's everybody's business." The fire flared up. The kid changed position, taking a seat on Maizie's carelessly thrown saddle. The coat, sagging because of the revolver in the pocket, flared open. Maizie stared, gasped.

"Why . . . you're a girl!"

The kid hastily covered her chest. "So there's two of us. Look at it this way: Duffy's after me, but he's got you."

"A girl. Runnin' around the country . . ."

"It doesn't matter. You're not going to take those guns to the Comanches."

"You're goin' to stop me." It was an assertion, not a question.

The kid swung the shotgun around, aiming it at the pack animal. "I'll blast it and the guns down into the river before I'll let you do it. You savvy?"

"And me with it. I savvy." Maizie showed no fear. She was staring at the maverick girl. She went on. "I know a couple of things, too. Antonio talks to me and me to him. I see things when my head's on straight."

"You don't know half of anything, you women from Duffy's."

"I can guess. I'm crazy about a man. You might as well know, the way things are. It's Soledad."

"The Comanche." The kid nodded. "That's why the guns."

"What about you?"

"Me? Are you altogether loco?" But the fire showed the flush that crept up from her throat to her cheeks.

"Cemetery Jones," said Maizie. "And they got him set up."

"They have, like hell. I busted him out of their rotten jail," said the kid. "And I'm stoppin' those guns from doin' him or his any harm."

"A man," said Maizie. "One man. Hell of a life, ain't it? You been runnin' wild on your own. Now it's a man. Me, I been wantin' my man for too long."

"Never mind about men," said the kid. "Right's right and wrong's wrong."

"Not where the man is, inside you, in your heart." Maizie shook her head. "You're just a baby." Her eyes flickered in the light of the fire as she looked over the kid's shoulder. Her mouth flew open.

The kid rolled. A shot clipped a twig as she fled with amazing speed for her mustang.

A man's voice said, "Drop the gun. Stop."

Maizie's voice cried, "Run, kid, run for your goddamn life."

Mac was on the mustang and galloping, still clinging somehow to the shotgun, leaning low, ducking her head to glance back. Maizie was standing between her and an Indian.

In another moment, she was swinging the horse down toward the river. This time she rode in the direction of the Crooked S ranch.

6

It was dawn and there was a stir in the bunkhouse. Sam had dreamed again. He always did after a shooting. He had never seen the man Max before. He had left him dead on the floor without a qualm, but dreams came to haunt him, now as before. He was sweating.

Francisco, his arm in a sling, was laying out various garments. Moseby was sitting on the edge of a bunk, ruefully regarding his tattered suit of black and white checks.

Francisco was saying, "Fella shouldn't wear rags like that anyhow, mister. Pick out what you can wear."

"That's real nice of you," said Moseby. "Is it time to arise?"

"Day's a-breakin'."

Sam said, "Good mornin', men."

"You was tossin' like a bull in heat," said Francisco. "You got a fever or somethin'?"

"No," said Sam shortly, trying to shrug off the dream.

"I'd better get ridin'," said the cowboy. "We're damn short-handed. Reckon this dude ain't here for chousin' cows."

"He don't even like cows," said Sam.

"Don't blame him. Ornery damn critters." Francisco, a fair-haired, red-cheeked youngster, grinned, showing a gap in his teeth. "I'll be moseyin' along. Pit'll be after me if I don't." He walked, bowlegged, from the bunkhouse."

Moseby said, "Fine folks hereabouts."

They had all talked the night before. Moseby and his rifle had been welcomed with open arms. They had kept the news from Mary, but they knew Duffy would move soon. There was only the threat of the Rangers to hold him now.

Sam began to dress. Moseby picked out a pair of Levis that fit him fairly well and a clean blue flannel shirt. He asked, "Could I wash up?"

"There's a pump and a trough. They got runnin' water in the kitchen sink. I'll be with you in a minute."

Sam sat on the edge of the bunk and pulled on his boots. The pressure was heavy upon him. He thought of Sunrise and Renee; he had never got off the letter to her that he had promised. He thought again of Duffy and that he could have killed the man and ended all of the problems. Nothing was going right, nothing had since he came to the Pecos.

Pit came to the door and beckoned. Sam joined him in the yard. Pit said, "You got to see somethin' you won't believe."

He led the way to the stable. In the farthest stall, there was a mustang nibbling at the few grains of oats it had not hitherto consumed. Saddle and blanket were draped over the partition.

Sam said, "So where's the damn kid?"

Pit pointed upward. "Sleepin' the sleep o' the just; it figures."

Sam climbed the ladder leading to the hayloft. The tiny figure was curled up, shotgun and machete by her side. She snored, coughed, woke up. Her face was not a foot from Sam's. She started; then for the first time since he had laid eyes on her, she smiled. It was a fleeting, little smile; immediately she was on her feet.

Sam said, "So. You finally got here."

"I slept too damn long." Her voice was hoarse. "I—I didn't want to come here. Then I knew I had to."

"It's about time. Get yourself together and come have some grub."

She went on. "I was out in the field, but I knew I had to come in and there was the horse. So I waited till everybody was asleep."

"Whatever," said Sam impatiently. "You're here, now. You've got to stay here."

She shook the last of sleep away. "I do, huh? Let me tell you, we better get goin' quick as quick. Maizie, that gal from Duffy's Place, has toted guns to the Indians."

"How do you know?"

"I followed her. They almost got me. . . . Never mind, I know where they are. We got to stop 'em."

"I'll say one thing for you, kid. You come straight to the point." He retreated down the ladder. He should have known, he thought, that things have to get worse before they get better. He watched the kid go to the pump and trough. Moseby was in the bunkhouse getting dressed. Pit was waiting at the kitchen door, and Matilda was behind him, arms akimbo, saying, "More vittles. Always more vittles."

Pit said, "Well, git to it, woman. Company. Make it plenty eggs and biscuits and ham."

Matilda vanished. Moseby came out of the bunkhouse, looked at the maverick kid, and raised his eyebrows.

Sam said, "It's the gal. Name of Mac. Don't ask any more."

"Certainly not, suh. Miss." He bowed. She scarcely glanced at him.

Sam said, "Into the house. Eat."

Moseby went. Sam stayed to watch Mac rinse beneath

the pump. She made quick work of it. He said, "You can tell it over breakfast."

She went obediently into the house. Matilda looked her up and down and asked, "How you like your egg, missy?"

"Now how in the devil did you know she was a girl?" demanded Sam.

"Any fool could see that," said Matilda. "You got no eyes? Jest look at her."

Pit, lounging against the door, said, "By Gawd, Sam. She's right. You look at her slanchways you can tell. We been blind as bats."

The girl was buttering biscuits and eating them, her eyes cast down.

Moseby said, "Now that you mention it, yes. I see. A mighty pretty gal, too."

The kid gave him a cold stare. "There's things to be done. Eat and get ready if you're man enough."

"Now don't you be hard on Mr. Moseby," Sam said. "He's a southern gentleman. He shoots a rifle."

Pit said, "You related to the Lamars, Mr. Moseby? Said that was your moniker, Lamar V. Right?"

"A cousin."

"Related to Mirabeau Bonaparte Lamar?"

"A great-uncle, I believe."

"Why, that man was at San Jacinto with Houston. Led the charge that chased Santa Anna to hell and gone. 'Twas the end of Santa Anna; gave us Texas."

"Matter of history," said Moseby. "No credit to me. One becomes a bit sick of hearing of him and L.Q.C."

"L.Q.C.?"

"Lucius Quintus Cincinnatis Lamar," said Sam. "From Mississippi. Great conciliator after the war. On the Supreme Court in Washington now, I do believe."

Pit said, "Why, man, that's one of the finest families in the country. You got to be proud."

Moseby sighed, shaking his head. "Suh, when one is

told that often enough, one runs away. I was heading for
California myself. Working my way, sort of."

Matilda said, "Eggs is ready. Ham comin' up. Them
Lamars, I heard of 'em. Owned slave ships."

"Ah," said Moseby, brightening. "That's more like it.
Bunch of damn crazy people with maddening Latin names.
Poets. Soldiers. Statesmen. Bah!"

Sam said, "The man means you can get mighty tired of
people tellin' you how to grow up, who you're supposed
to be."

The kid chewed, swallowed, then said, "You better eat
up and be ready. Those Comanches got guns, I tell you.
That Maizie, she's in love with Soledad. He almost killed
me. They want horses. You got horses here. Duffy sent
'em the guns."

Sam said, "The kid's right."

"You goin' to leave here again, Sam?" Pickens asked.

"Duffy needs a bit more time. Those damn Comanches
could come down and burn and kill or at least steal the
horses. Think on it, Pit. First things first."

The kid called Mac stopped eating and stared at Sam.

"I could've killed Duffy last night. When I started the
fire."

"I could've got him, too, kid," Sam said softly. "Just
eat and get ready, and we'll go."

Moseby said, "Not without me, suh."

"Okay."

Pit hesitated at the door. "You people. All three. You're
here to save our bacon. God bless."

He vanished before they could reply. There was nothing
to say in any case, Sam thought. A waif, a gambler, and
he who owed a debt, they had come together. Also, the
job was far from accomplished.

As they were leaving, Matilda brought sandwiches. She
said, "The good Lawd knows I got no love for southern-

ers. But when you go out for my folks, I bless you with all my heart.''

''Thank you, Matilda,'' said Moseby. ''Me, I never owned a slave, but my relatives did. Some were in the Klan, but that was durin' Reconstruction when the Kluxers did some good. Me, I'm a sort of renegade.''

''You're in Texas where nobody asks about your past,'' Sam told him. ''Let's get out of here.''

The horses were saddled; the mustang, a black for Moseby, and Junior. Moseby slung his rifle to the saddle and said, ''Me huntin' Indians. Now who in the world would believe it? I can't.''

''Believe it,'' Sam said. ''And watch your head. Injuns ain't great shots, but they get lucky sometimes.''

They rode, the mustang slightly in the lead, silent against the possibilities of the near future.

Sam nudged the roan alongside the mustang. ''Kid, why don't you tell us your real name and what you got against Duffy and all?''

She shook her head and the stubborn expression he remembered settled in. ''No.''

''You got to, sooner or later.''

''Later,'' she said. ''When it's done.''

''When what's done?''

She stared at him. ''When Duffy's dead.''

She clapped heels to the mustang and darted ahead. Sam pursed his lips, then shook his head. ''That gal. She's got me wonderin' in circles.''

''In Texas they don't ask questions,'' Moseby reminded him.

''Go to hell,'' said Sam. They rode on, down by the river, then up a trail that made them ride single file to the top of the bluff where Maizie had made camp.

The kid said, ''There's a higher point. They're in a ravine. We'll get high gun on 'em.''

''How many of them?'' asked Sam.

"Not as many as people think," she replied. "Best leave the horses."

They tied up and went afoot, the girl in the lead. Sam turned over in his mind the several ways to handle the deal. They were outnumbered, but if they had surprise and high gun it might work. He knew the language, but making them listen was another matter. They were young braves, and the moon raid was near at hand and they would be touchy.

Suddenly his eye caught movement ahead and he hissed, "Stop!"

They crouched down. He motioned to them to remain still and went ahead, prowling, silent as a snake in the grass. The Comanches might have a sentinel. He circled off the narrow trail and crept back. He had the rifle ready to use as a bludgeon. He saw movement and sprang.

A quiet voice said, "Dammit, Jones, you like to scare me clean to pieces."

"Keen."

The Ranger crawled into view.

"How many?" Sam asked.

"A dozen, and Soledad. And a whore."

"I know about the woman. She close with 'em?"

"Too close. She and Soledad are real damn close. The others, they got their noses up their asses. I been watchin'. Was about to go send a telegram. I ain't no hero."

"There's three of us."

"Makes a difference. You got any ideas?"

"Nope. Rather look-see first off," Sam told him.

"Tell your people not to shoot," Keen said. "It ain't strictly business, but I gotta go along with you."

"You can go on to town."

Keen grinned at him. "Can't take a joke, huh, Jones?"

"Lead us up there."

Sam went back and brought the others. They walked in silence in the tracks of the Ranger. They came to the edge of the canyon and looked down. There was a small fire and the Comanches were lounging. Sitting apart were Maizie and Soledad. The tension among them was visible even at a distance. Braves talked behind their hands, staring at the man and the woman. The guns and ammunition were neatly stacked. Maizie seemed to be talking a blue streak to Soledad, who listened stone-faced.

The rope corral in which they kept their mangy horses was at the narrow end of the canyon, between the Indians and the entrance below.

Sam said to Keen, whispering, "You see what I see?"

"Could be."

"Let me palaver. If it don't work, try what we're thinkin'."

"It'll be a small war. The kid?"

"Trust me," said Sam.

"Your deal." The Ranger vanished in the direction of the blind end of the canyon. He was good, Sam thought, damn good. He moved like a ghost and with startling speed.

Sam found a spot behind some heavy brush, where he could be heard but not seen. He called in Comanche, "Braves! Do not move. You are surrounded."

They started to their feet. Sam fired the rifle into the air and repeated, "We do not want to fight. We want to parley."

Soledad separated himself from Maizie and stepped forward. "Who are you that speaks our tongue and wants to parley?"

"Sam Jones."

Maizie said, "That is the man I told you about."

"I fear no man." Soledad folded his arms and stood tall.

One of the braves shouted. Others joined in. Some did not, Sam noted. He said out of the corner of his mouth, "Spread out. Don't let 'em get to the guns."

The pack animal stood at the end of the ravine, nibbling at foliage. In the corral of sagging rope, the horses of the Comanches stood with heads hung, oblivious.

Sam called, "We do not want you to be afraid. We want to talk to you about raiding the Crooked S."

"That is our business." Soledad was defiant to the core.

One of the Indians began crawling toward the stacked rifles. He was small and slim, and he maneuvered so that the bodies of others sheltered him. There was no way to get a clean shot to deter him without killing or wounding another brave.

Sam said, "It is our business also. The man Duffy will not reward you. In the end you will have to fight him and all his gunmen."

"He's right," Maizie said.

Soledad said, "We need horses. Will you give us horses?"

"They are not mine to give," Sam told him.

"Then we will take them if we live."

The brave who was snaking his way to the rifles reached his goal. There was the sound of a shot. The bullet struck, not the Indian, but the stacked guns, toppling them. The Comanche rolled away, unhurt.

Sam said, "You see? We could have killed him." It was Moseby who had fired the shot, he knew. The southerner had not been boasting idly of his marksmanship.

Soledad said, "You have killed many of us. We still have no fear. We must have horses."

The Comanche leader was weakening, Sam realized. There was a deal in the making. "If we give you good horses, will you go on the moon raid?"

He could see Soledad wavering. There were horses to spare in the Crooked S corral. It would be worthwhile to trade them for security against a Comanche raid. Sam temporized.

"I will talk with the man who owns the horses," he said. "You will come with me. I swear to your safety."

Maizie urged, "You can trust him. He is Cemetery Jones."

It was a trepidatious moment. Sam felt a surge of optimism. Then two braves shouted, "No! No!"

One of them made a dash for the guns. Sam fired close enough to send him tumbling unhurt to earth. Moseby followed suit.

"We do not wish to hurt you," Sam shouted.

The moment had passed. There was a movement by the dissidents among the Comanches. In another few seconds there would be a small war.

Then Ranger Keen came thundering in, swinging a whip, howling. He slammed into the rope corral and set free the Comanche horses. He drove them through the scattering braves and out the narrow end of the canyon.

There was complete confusion. Sam said, "This is no damn good," and slid down the sloping edge of the ravine. Soledad spun around, undecided, unarmed. His men huddled, not understanding.

Keen yelled, "Round 'em up."

In that second, his horse stepped into a hole. He went up and over and down. He lay still as a stone as his horse recovered, shivered, and stood stock-still.

Sam held his rifle on Soledad. He said, "My men will cut you down, every last one of you, unless you listen."

Sweat was running down his back. If Soledad guessed how few they were, it was all over, he knew. He prayed they would not show themselves, the kid and the southern marksman. It was now a poker game and he held his only card open and on the table: the rifle in his hands, the muzzle pressed against the chest of the Indian. It was time for bluffing.

He said loudly and angrily, "That man you have caused to die is a Texas Ranger. You know what that means. Not one of you will make another moon raid. They will track you down and destroy you.'' He sought words in their peculiar patois. ''You are brave, but you are foolish. Maizie.''

She jumped as though stuck with a knife point.

He said, ''Load those rifles and the ammunition onto that pack animal. Jump!''

She obeyed without hesitation. She had enough know-how to stack the weapons in the panniers, Sam saw. Then, out of the corner of his eye, he caught movement among the recalcitrants he had noticed before. They were moving toward Maizie.

He called, ''Moseby! Come down here. You others stay.''

Moseby came sliding. The Comanches hesitated, then charged. Moseby fired two shots.

There was a howl and a scream. One Indian doubled over with a broken shinbone. The other whirled around clapping his left hand to his right shoulder.

Soledad twitched, but Sam thrust the muzzle of the rifle into his belly. ''Foolish. Don't you be foolish. Tell your men to obey.''

Soledad hesitated. Moseby menaced the braves who made spasmodic movement. Sam thought of the kid up on the edge of the canyon with only her shotgun and her machete. The whole endeavor hung by a thread. If Soledad was fanatic enough to die, there was no chance they could survive a concerted attack by the remaining Comanches.

Moseby was reloading. There was a light in his eyes that Sam had not seen before. The Comanches were huddling, staring. Sam asked, ''Everyone up top okay?''

''Yes, suh,'' said Moseby calmly. ''Doin' just fine.''

Sam said, ''Take my place here. If he moves, kill him.''

Moseby walked slowly to them and thrust his rifle muzzle into Soledad's chest, looked him in the eye, and said, "You heard the man."

Soledad blinked. Maizie continued to stack rifles. Sam checked her and nodded. "We'll get you out of this."

"I don't want out. I want to be with him."

"Whatever," said Sam. "Just do like I say now."

He walked to where Ranger Keen lay. He bent down and Keen opened one eye. Sam slowly shook his head. "So he's dead. There's only one way you can survive now, Soledad, without the Rangers on your back, that is. Do you savvy? Only if we live to tell that it was an accident."

After a short moment, Soledad nodded. He said hoarsely, "You would leave us without our horses?"

"We didn't start this," Sam said. "You can track the horses; we will not steal them. You cannot have the guns."

Brave and quick in action these Indians were, but Sam knew that they could be mesmerized by a succession of events not previously in their experience. He counted upon this knowledge now. He said smoothly, "Maizie, empty those rifles that you brought."

She did so, spilling the cartridges on the ground. Soledad shook his head in despair.

Sam spoke again. "Now toss the ammunition into the bushes over yonder."

Again she did as she was told. It was getting closer and closer to danger time. Everything depended on timing. Well, thought Sam, didn't all else in this world depend on it? He grinned at Soledad.

"You have men to care for. You have horses to track. Not one of yours has died here, and we would like it to remain so. Our quarrel is with Duffy, not with the Comanche," Sam said. In almost the same breath, he threw over his shoulder to Moseby, "Load that Ranger on his horse, and do it respectful-like."

It had all happened too fast for Soledad to absorb the events, but he knew he had been foiled for the present. He grunted and muttered, almost to himself, "I will remember you, Cemetery Jones."

"Good," came Sam's quick riposte. "Then remember that I saved your life!"

"Pah!"

"And remember that I leave you your woman. That we did not come to kill. The death of the Ranger was no fault of yours. Pray to your gods that I live to testify in court as to your innocence." Sam could not be sure that he had translated all so that Soledad could understand it, but he knew the Comanche had the gist of it.

It was still devilishly ticklish, and Sam stepped away with an air of assurance that he wished he could truly feel. He followed Moseby and the horse bearing the Ranger. He walked backward, very carefully. It was a good piece to the mouth of the ravine. One misstep and there was no way to predict what the Comanches might do. Aroused from their trance, they might make a rush, taking their chances on death from the muzzle of his gun. They had been known to do much worse.

Sam called back as he retreated, "Maizie, tell him Duffy will be ridin' on the Crooked S. Tell him Duffy wants it all, everything in the county. Ask him if he thinks Duffy will do more for him than Stubby." It was one more chance to take today.

Maizie nodded and slapped the pack animal onto the trail toward him. Sam picked up the lead line in his left hand. He knew he would have to be extra careful since the Comanches wanted the rifles so badly that they would take almost any chance. One of them moved and Sam fired from the hip, missing the Indian by a hair. Soledad's eyes glittered in fury, but he motioned the Comanche group to complete stillness.

Sam went on. His heel hit a rock and he stumbled over a tricky place in the path but managed to keep his rifle steady. The Comanches leaned forward as though on leashes, then swayed back as they looked into the face of certain death.

The trail, scarcely visible, ran narrow through the canyon. Only the kid knew its eccentricity. Moseby led the little caravan carefully, with the Ranger facedown on his horse. In pain as he must be, Keen gave no sign of life for the Comanches to read. It was important that they believe that the Ranger was dead. The little caravan crept along, step by step. With the utmost concentration, Sam kept his eyes on the back trail.

When they came to a wider place, there was also the danger of Duffy's men prowling the area. When Sam felt that the Indians had followed them no farther, he made his way to Keen. The Ranger's eyes were closed, his face rigid with pain. The horse was remarkably steady, a well-trained animal.

Sam asked, "Can you make it?"

"Got to," muttered Keen through clenched teeth.

"The doctor will come right out to the ranch," Sam told him. "Stay tough."

"It ain't easy. My damn hip."

There was a lump on his head as well. Sam realized the Ranger had suffered a concussion in the fall. "Can you handle it for a while?"

"Got to, don't I?"

"Think you can set the saddle?"

"My hip." He seemed to drift away. Moseby came, and they tried to make him comfortable.

The kid suddenly appeared. Impatient, she said, "I got rid of the Comanche who was following. Now I got to get our horses."

"Yeah." She was gone before Sam could draw a breath. He said to Moseby, "She's right sudden."

Moseby was staring after her. "Who in Sam Hill is she?"

"That's somethin' we don't know and wish we did. Calls herself Mac; hates Duffy."

"Beautiful girl," said Moseby.

"You noticed that? Dangerous as a rattler. Mean as a mule." Sam shook his head. "Good as gold, and maybe brighter."

They made their way slowly along the uncertain path. Sam knew the kid had to climb to the bluff, mount, and lead horses that hated to be led. That she could do so was a matter of course. Still, there was danger everywhere.

They plodded along. Sam said, "You looked mighty fine back there, podner. What do you call yourself among friends?"

"Checkers'll do, suh." He smiled. "Never been in such a fuss before. Wouldn't have believed I could manage."

"You can shoot with anybody hereabouts. And elsewhere."

"Shootin', sure, that's one thing. Firin' at people you don't know, that's another. Scary business."

They came to a place where longhorns munched placidly on grass. Sam said, "There's your cows."

"Never took note of them before," said Moseby. "Long-legged critters, ain't they."

"They can run, and you better not be sittin' still in their way when they decide to go," Sam told him. "You won't know scared till you been in a stampede."

"I'll keep that in mind." Moseby walked on a few steps silently, then said, "Only wanted to get to California, y'know? All this is outa my line."

"Tell you the truth, it ain't what you might call a reg'lar sort of happenstance. Comes about when a man gets too greedy and reaches too far."

"Duffy?"

"There's been others. Some of 'em own thousands of acres, sit in high places."

"Could be stopped, you reckon?"

"Aim to try," Sam told him.

"Seems worthwhile." Moseby was making a commitment. It was apparent in his voice and his grin. "You notice that gal toted her blunderbuss along with her?"

"What you didn't see is, she carries a machete strung down her back." Sam grinned. "Nobody catches her short."

"A magnolia blossom she's not, for sure. But some kind of a gal, she certainly is," said Moseby.

"For sure," Sam answered. He wondered if Renee, back in Sunrise, would, in all her wisdom, be able to give him a notion about little Mac and what made her tick.

They reached a stand of pine near the main road leading to Stubby's place. They stopped, and Sam again checked the Ranger. There was no sign of the kid and the horses.

Keen moaned, a low, deep note. Between them, Sam and Moseby managed to ease him down from the horse to a clump of soft, fallen needles. He opened his eyes and murmured, "My damn hip."

Sam examined his right hip gingerly. Moseby looked over his shoulder and said apologetically, "I've had a bit of trainin' in this, suh."

"Good. What can we do?"

"If you'll hold him steady."

Sam did so. Moseby explored with his gambler's hands. He loosened the Ranger's belt, pushed against bone. There was a somewhat frightening click, and then Keen's body patently relaxed. The Ranger sighed and slept for the first time.

"You did that right smart," Sam said. He asked no questions, he was proffered no explanation. He was becoming aware of the depths within depths in Lamar V. Moseby, alias Checkers. "Good thing, too. I was lyin' about the doctor. It'll be more like a week."

"This one'll be laid up that long at least," Moseby said.

"He's tough." Sam explained, "All Rangers are tough hombres. Born that way, seems like. Poor pay; life's never their own; people shootin' at 'em. People like Duffy. Indians. Mexican bandits raidin' across the Rio Grande. Not many of 'em, these Rangers, but they get a lot of respect.''

''Respect. Ah, yes.''

Sam noted the wistful note in Moseby's voice. ''Give 'em cause, they'd be down on Duffy right sudden. Keen, here, he was assigned to the Comanches, so he stuck to it. Still, Duffy knows he's around; it slows him down.''

''You reckon Duffy will move if he knows Keen is out of it?''

''Long as he don't know just where Keen is, it might keep him worried at least.''

Moseby said, ''Duffy's got the army, Duffy's got the money, Duffy's got the desire. You sure we ain't fightin' the War Between the States all over again—on the wrong side?''

''Hell, no! I ain't sure of doodley squat,'' said Sam. ''Although seems like we don't always get to choose the side we might like in most wars. Hell!'' He swore admiringly. ''Here comes that wild kid.''

She was hunched over the neck of the mustang as always. She had not found it necessary to lead the roan or the black; they were trotting alongside her, doing her bidding.

Moseby said, ''Extraordinary.''

''Whatever. Goes beyond reason. Loco kid.''

Moseby politely disagreed, with raised eyebrows. ''Beautiful child. Nature's own, perhaps.''

She came in and looked down at the Ranger. ''He goin' to die?''

''No. He's goin' to Stubby's house,'' Sam said.

She said, ''Didn't see hair nor hide of any of Duffy's riders. Can you figure what that means?''

''Could be a gathering,'' said Sam. ''Let's get on the road.''

"I'll go into town."

Sam said, "No."

"I can learn what's goin' to happen," she argued.

"We know what's goin' to happen," Sam told her. "We just don't know when. You go with us."

"Please?" Moseby added.

She ignored him. Her big eyes fixed on Sam intently. "You mean it, don't you?"

"You better believe it."

For a moment she hesitated. Then she said in a smaller voice, "If you really, damn, truly mean it."

"It's for the good of all of us."

"If you say so."

Sam heard the compliance in her voice with relief. He said, "Let's get the Ranger back to the Crooked S. Time's a-wastin'."

It was the first time the kid had given an inch. Sam wondered if she was obeying him or if it had been Moseby's placating "please" that had swayed her. He would, he grudgingly concluded, never understand this maverick girl.

They made their way slowly. They passed a herd of longhorns being watched by a couple of Stubby's men. The skies were darkening. A Texas storm was suddenly threatening. The cowboys were riding among the cattle humming to the sensitive, hairy ears. Storms were often the cause of stampedes and soothing sounds seldom stopped them, Sam knew.

At the ranch, Pit Pickens was waiting. He asked, "You see Callahan and Casey on the way? Sent 'em to watch out for the storm."

"Didn't see them, just Morgan and Dobey," said Sam. "Give us a hand with the Ranger here."

Pit came to help, asking no questions. He said, "Got no place but the bunkhouse." He nodded toward Mac. "She goes in the house."

"Just let's get him comfortable," said Sam.

They made up a corner bunk for Keen. He muttered unintelligible sentences, then said clearly, "Wish to report. Soledad and band in canyon . . . Horses . . ." He lapsed back into limbo.

"Fever," said Pickens. "Got to give him somethin'. By golly, look at the lump on his head."

"The rock was harder," Sam said. He looked at the girl. "You go inside the house. This here is for men."

"Men don't scare me." She snorted.

"Scarin' ain't it," he told her.

Pickens spoke. "Just when I got it all sorted out . . . Will somebody tell me what's been goin' on?"

"First and foremost, we're all hungry," Sam said. "If you can look after this Ranger, maybe Matilda will put on some grub for us."

"Matilda can look out for the . . . Ranger, you say?" Pit answered. "I got to know what's goin' on."

They went into the kitchen. Matilda said, "Pot's on. What you all want of me now?"

"Man out yonder's got a fever," Pit said. "You know what to do."

"What man?" Matilda was suspicious.

"A Texas Ranger," Sam said. "Fell on his head."

"Hmph! If more white folks fell on their heads, might knock some sense into 'em." Nevertheless, she gathered towels, mustard, and other ingredients known to every ranch dweller and made her way out to the bunkhouse.

Pickens said, "Stubby's out lookin' for trouble. Is he going to find it right now, or later, is what I want to know."

"Who can tell? The Comanches are lookin' for their horses. We got a load of guns Duffy intended for them. Storm's comin' up, and the Ranger's got a headache," Sam answered.

Moseby added, "If I might say so, you've got another man to fight for you."

"Good news, bad news, news that don't mean nothin'," said Pickens. "Mary's pinin'. She don't truly know what's happenin', but, hell, she can guess."

He went to a shelf and took down some earthen bowls. He took the lid off a huge pot set on the back of the wood-burning stove and a heavy aroma filled the air. He reached for a ladle hanging on the wall and began dishing out portions for each of them. He said, "Lord only knows what's in this, but it's been cookin' steady since Matilda came here. She says pore people allus keep somethin' like it. Anything left over, seems like, goes into it."

They all tasted gingerly at first but then ate the tasty stew with great relish. They heard a sound without, and Pickens said, "Stubby. He can't stay away from Mary long enough to swat a fly."

Stubby came into the kitchen. He said, "Pack animal. Bunch of guns and stuff. What the hell?" He looked at the kid and said, " 'Scuse me. I keep forgettin'."

"Keep right on," Mac said with her mouth full.

Sam said, "Duffy's stuff for the Comanches. Meant to swap some of your corral to them today." He grinned. "Didn't work out, so we took the guns."

"Where's Matilda?" Stubby asked. "She should be lookin' after Mary. Sure as hell it's goin' to storm. Everything's goin' haywire." Stubby was tightly strung. "If the cows start for the river, I dunno what'll happen."

"Whatever," Sam said. "Best we should all get a bit of sleep. You want to show the kid here where she can bunk?"

Stubby brightened appreciably at the thought of something he could take charge of immediately. "Sure I can," he said, grinning at the kid. "Mary'll want to see you, for sure!"

The kid turned to Sam, her eyes wide with panic.

Sam nailed her with a look. "You might as well get

used to it. There're ladies in this world. Not Maizies, ladies." He measured the last word.

The kid responded quickly. "You think I don't know anything? Huh? Anyway, Maizie ain't all bad—she kept that crazy Comanche from blowing off my head, didn't she?" Mac's voice gave the tiniest quaver. "You . . . You . . . Sam Jones. . . ." Her voice trailed off, and her mouth shut tight again, little lines of bitterness showing at the corners.

Sam said gently, "It ain't like I didn't ask, is it, kid?"

She shook her head. Sam shrugged. Stubby looked from one to the other without understanding. Moseby started to speak, cleared his throat, then decided against it.

In the silence, Mary's voice could be heard calling. Stubby started as if shot and ran for the stairway.

Pit said, "Best we wait before we go up now."

Matilda entered from outdoors, saying, "Whoooeee! It's sure comin' up to storm."

Sam asked, "Matilda, tell me somethin'. Is Mary in pain or anything? I mean, is she poorly?"

"Lawsy me, no. Mens ain't got a lick of sense when it comes to women havin' babies. Animals, they know about. Womens, they're scared over nothin'."

"She's right," said Pickens. "How's the Ranger?"

"Poorly. But he gonna live. He just needs some sleepy time," said Matilda. "I give him some remedy. Now what about this one here? She sure needs some clean clothes."

Pickens said, "You know what? She's about the size that Mary was years agone, 'fore you even came here. Why don't you see what you can find."

"I don't want no handouts," the kid began. Then she looked at Sam and stopped. "I could sure use some sleep, though."

"We all could. But it seems like Mary might want to know a few things," Sam said.

Mac said, "I'm scared, Sam."

Stubby's voice echoed in the stairwell. "Sam, bring up the kid, huh?"

"Coming," Sam said, and noticed that Matilda had her in a firm grip.

Mac said, flinching, "No. I'm too—I don't look right."

Sam said, "You could take that machete off. Maybe your coat?"

She clung to the oversized jacket, although she allowed Matilda to take the machete. "I don't . . . I haven't got a camisole." Her voice was a whisper as Matilda removed the coat.

"We noticed," said Sam. "You think Mary's gonna care?"

The kid gave up her struggle reluctantly, never taking her eyes off Sam. Matilda let Mac go and she went slowly ahead of him, taking one stair step at a time. Stubby waited at the top, his face showing relief, pleasure, and curiosity all at the same time.

They went into Mary's room. She took one look at the frightened, embarrassed girl and said, "All right now, you men get. Leave this to us ladies." She indicated to Matilda that she should remain. Mary was sitting up, propped up by pillows, radiant, smiling. The girl went, without hesitation now, to the side of the bed.

Sam said, "You're lookin' right pert, Miz Stone."

"You get some rest now," she said. "Both of you. Matilda and me, we'll take care of this." She reached out a hand to the girl. The men moved to obey, and she added, "Shut that door behind you."

In the hallway, Sam said, "A good day for her?"

"She always perks right up durin' a storm," said Stubby. "Rain, thunder, lightnin', it makes her feel good."

Downstairs, they sat at the table, drank Matilda's good coffee, and went over details of the day. Rain began to fall.

Sam concluded, "On the way back I got a feelin', like someone was watchin' us."

Stubby said, "That would be that son of a bitch, Ed Fielder. You mind I told you he went over? Stole my spyglass. You remember my spyglass, Sam."

"Your old man's, right? From when he went to sea?"

"Right. That Fielder's a slimy rat. Raked him over the coals for foolin' with Matilda. He quit without his pay."

"Took your glass with him, didn't he? And Duffy pays."

"A-plenty." Stubby looked up at Moseby, his earlier exuberance dissipated. "You goin' to join up? I'll sure pay."

"Not necessary," Moseby told him. "Your friend here yanked me out of durance vile. Besides which, suh, I need a fight. It's been too long."

Sam grinned. "All you rebels only need a cause. It's in your blood, way I see it."

"Duffy," said Moseby. "He's cause enough for any man, I believe."

Sam squinted at him. "You said it's been too long. Thought you weren't in the war?"

"No, I was too young, and apprenticed to the only doctor in three counties. Mine was a feud. You know about southern family feuds?"

"Hell, we got 'em here," said Pickens.

Moseby bowed elegantly. "Well, that was the reason for my departure from Alabama. I was the better rifle shot."

Sam shook his head. "It always comes to that for some. Killin'. That fellow Max—had to kill him. Had to get outa jail before they killed us. Don't make it go down any easier, does it?"

Moseby looked away and said slowly, "He was my cousin, the one I killed."

Pit made a wide gesture. "C'mon now. Duffy ain't nobody's cousin."

Still, Sam wished he could talk to Renee. He knew she would be worrying now because he had not sent the promised letter. She would be playing the solemn music, and the customers would listen but not feel like dancing, although they wouldn't understand why, and business in El Sol would fall off. There was always something. He made himself concentrate on the ways to handle Duffy.

None of them heard Mary's muffled exclamation from above except for the kid and Matilda, who were in her room.

"Don't tell Stubby and Sam," Mary said, grabbing a hand on either side of the bed. "Don't tell," she said urgently as she was caught in another welcome, healthy, early spasm. She grinned happily, conspiratorially.

7

The man named Ed Fielder had a cast in his left eye, a sharp nose, and a bad complexion. He sat in Duffy's office and said with assurance, " 'Course I know. I know every damn inch of this here country. I seen 'em. I had my spyglass."

"Ah, yes, me boy. So the Ranger is dead?" Duffy asked.

"Deader'n a mackerel. Lyin' across the saddle. Never moved an inch. Just danglin'."

"And the rains come," mused Duffy. "Ah, have a touch of the whiskey, man." He poured generously into a tumbler.

Fielder drank eagerly. "I'll be the foreman, you said."

"Of course, me boy." It was a good thing Jackson wasn't in the room, Duffy thought. Magrew and Jackson would be another problem once it was all settled. Maybe he could depend on Cemetery Jones to dispatch them, as they dispatched him.

"Let that be a secret between us, now. Remember that," Duffy said aloud.

"I know. Some of them are jealous." Fielder thought he knew more than the others. He had always thought himself denied his rightful place in the world. Stubby Stone had never recognized his ability. As for that black woman . . . Well, he would see about her, too, when the time came.

Duffy said, "This storm, now. There must be a way to put it to our advantage." He paused, then said, "You say the raggedy kid was with them?"

"I seen him with 'em. That was when they was fightin' the Injuns."

"And Maizie?"

"Couldn't get close enough to spot her. I know she went to the Comanches with the guns."

"I see." Duffy did not see and he did not understand. Maizie should have been back before now with the glad news that the Comanches would attack the Crooked S and steal the horses. Well, the rain, he thought. It was coming down pretty heavy, and there was lightning and thunder and all that.

Fielder said, "Y'know the cattle get awful damn skittish in a storm like this one comin' up."

"Yes."

"Your own herd, now. It could stampede."

"I've got riders out there." More were coming in, he knew, a few Mexicans vaqueros, the best there were.

"You're sure about the Indians? Maizie got there?" Duffy asked again.

"That's all I know." Fielder had been scared to go closer. He had maintained a safe distance from Maizie and the braves. His scalp tingled every time he thought about Comanches. "The cattle, now. That's what I know best. I could go out there and straw-boss the riders."

"Ah, now, why don't you do that, m'boy? You find Madero. You tell him I sent you to take charge."

"Sure! Where'll I find him?"

Duffy waved a hand. "Somewhere on my property. You know the land, you said. Look for him, m'boy."

"Sure. Well. Okay." Fielder finished his drink and started for the door. "Uh, everything's okay, right?"

"Okay? Everything never is okay. Tell me again about that damned kid."

"Well, I seen her talkin' to Maizie." Fielder swallowed, his Adam's apple bobbing. He had been a safe distance from that scene. "Her and Maizie. Then I seen her again with Jones and the pack animal, goin' toward the Crooked S."

"A pack animal. What was the pack animal carryin'?"

"That I couldn't say."

"I see. So. Go to Madero. On the way out, tell Jackson and Magrew I want to talk with 'em."

The pack animal could be the one carrying the guns, Duffy thought. If Maizie and the kid . . . The damned spy, Fielder, was a no-good skunk, a traitor of no talent except to nose about from afar. Besides which he was a liar when he could get away with it.

Now the question was, what about the Comanches? Maizie could be taken care of later. The laudanum could be used to do her in, the little bitch. No matter what, she had no business conniving with the damned kid. He wanted that kid as he had not wanted anyone in all his life. He wanted her alive.

Fielder had his uses. He had made a plan of the house and yard at the Crooked S. There were ways to attack it if it came to that. Enough men, enough fire power, and any ranch could be taken—lock, stock, and barrel. With the Ranger dead, it had to be successful if it was done quickly enough.

Thunder sounded and lightning flashed. It was a night for action if he could put it all together as he had planned. Jackson and Magrew, he needed them more than they knew. He needed them to take care of Cemetery Jones.

The gunmen came into the office. Duffy said, "Ah, me two top hands. Have a touch now, do." He poured whiskey for them. They regarded him without speaking. He said, "Tonight, I do believe. Do ye agree?"

Magrew shrugged, silent as usual. Jackson tossed down the booze and said, "What you got in mind, Duffy?"

"They'll be watchin' the cattle, won't they, now? We've got Madero and his banditos watchin' ours."

Jackson said, "Reckon they will. It's a night for keepin' the herds quiet."

Duffy spread out the sketch Fielder had made atop his desk. "This is the way it stands, me boys. You see? It's a strong house. But it has spots where it can be struck. Take a few of your men, get in close, and strike hard and fast."

Jackson looked at the drawing. "You aim to kill all them people?"

"Oh, no, indeed. Just to make them see the light. Jones, of course. Jones will have to go."

"And that's our job."

Duffy said, "A thousand dollars apiece above your pay if you get him."

"And his cemetery if we don't."

"You hired on," Duffy reminded him. "You knew I had to have the Crooked S to tie together what I want."

Magrew drained his glass and helped himself to more whiskey. Jackson stared at Duffy.

"There's a woman goin' to have a baby out there. Fightin's one thing. Murder, that's another."

Duffy forced a laugh. "Murder, he says. Jones has already wounded Johnson and killed Max Kelsey altogether. Why else do they call him 'Cemetery'? How can ye murder a man of his ken?"

"I'm talkin' about the woman. And what of the maverick kid you want so bad?"

"The kid's out there with 'em, I tell ye. The women are not to be harmed. I'll kill anyone hurts the kid meself."

"Then you're ridin' with us?" There was a touch of sarcasm in Jackson's voice.

Duffy looked at him for a long moment. Then he said, "So that's it. You're thinkin' because I hire scum like you that I'm scared?"

He whipped a gun out of his desk drawer. Jackson and Magrew blinked at the sudden move.

Duffy said, "Try me."

For a moment, it hung in the balance. Then Jackson threw his hands out and said, "So you're ready."

"I didn't get where I am by being a coward," Duffy told him. "If you live long enough, you'll know when to hire and when to do. The time has come for me to do. I'm ridin'."

Magrew spoke suddenly. "And if you get it, who pays us?"

"Ah, now, y'see? There's always that. Look at it this way. If they get me, all is lost, so ye come back here and take what you can find and hightail it for Mexico. What else? Ye know the way it is in a war. Winners take all, losers take what they can get."

"The man's right," said Jackson. "We hired on and it comes down to gettin' Jones. Which is what we almost did, but we lost him. Now it's fish or cut bait."

"Now you're talkin'. So go, lads, and we'll meet at the livery stable."

"We won't leave without you," said Jackson.

Alone, Duffy went to a closet that occupied most of one wall. He slid back the creaking doors. His wardrobe was part of his pride; it contained an outfit for any occasion. He touched the finery from Mexico that he loved. There was the gold brocade jacket that his wife had given him, the poor, miserable woman. He shrugged and then from the shelf took a black sombrero to fit the weather and a long, divided slicker he had had made for him.

It had been a hard life at times, mainly in the scheming, he thought, smiling to himself. The greatest lesson he had learned was to have others do for him. They were mainly fools and he used them. Stubby Stone had been the easiest of them all. For a fleeting second, he felt pity for the woman Stubby had married, then he shrugged again. All women were to be used; they were decorative and pleasing to the touch, and that was it. They produced offspring, but he had no desire to propagate himself.

He was his own man, he boasted to himself. Self-made, self-contained, he was the master. With his wits and his drive for power, he would prevail, as had the giants of Texas before him. They had all swung a wide loop; they had all been robber barons in the beginning. He would be one of them and sit in high places, and Bowville would be his headquarters, his town in the Pecos country. He would be a king.

It would be easy, too, were it not for that damned Cemetery Jones. Duffy buckled on his gun belt, donned the slicker, and went to have Simon bring his horse. Simon, the fool of fools, was his weakness, he admitted to himself. The gunmen and the riders worked for pay and kept a certain prideful independence. Simon was another matter, a bumbling slave. He had only to nod and Simon would rush eagerly to serve him. He needed a Simon.

There were few customers in the saloon, only the poker players, a few heavy drinkers, and Simon. Duffy grandly ordered drinks on the house and waved Simon on his errand. He stood at the end of the bar, drank a double whiskey, and prepared himself to ride into the elements.

In the town of Sunrise, the weather was clear, the stage came in on time, the jail was devoid of prisoners, and the eternal poker game for low stakes among the town councilmen went on and on in the saloon known as El Sol. Donkey Donovan came to Renee, who was at the piano, with a long face.

"No mail," he said.

"He's in trouble." Renee played Chopin with a beat of her own.

"He can always get outa trouble," said the marshal.

"He cannot get to the post office," said Renee. "That means deep trouble."

"No news is good news?" Donkey tried to smile.

"Not in this case," she said. There were hollows beneath her eyes. "I have a sad feeling about this. I wish I could dissipate this feeling."

Donkey said, "Sam never loses, you know that."

"It's really not his life for which I fear." Her voice was very quiet. "It's his soul."

"Aw. Please don't fret, Renee." Donkey touched her shoulder.

He understood vaguely. "Maybe you'd like to see the preacher."

She forced a smile. "The preacher and I have talked."

"He's a good man."

"In his fashion," she murmured. Preacher Shawn was a bit too holy for her taste, too strong on fundamentals and too weak on subtleties of the faith. "He is good for the town. I prefer talking with Abe Solomon. He is a wise man."

Solomon was the town banker, a founding father, and close to Sam Jones and Renee. His wisdom was always a balm to her fears.

As she thought of him, gray-bearded Abe Solomon entered the saloon accompanied by large, young Adam Burr, a thoroughly transplanted Eastern youth, and his bride, the former Peggy McLane. They gathered around the piano and frowned when Renee shook her head.

"But he promised to write," said Peggy McLane Burr.

"That, my dear, is the point," said her husband. "Sam always keeps his promises."

"I know that." Peggy frowned. "Maybe he's just awful busy. Maybe there's no pen and paper where he is."

Solomon, the wise, said, "Maybe the moon is made of green cheese. We all know he's into something, no?"

"Yes. A lot of something," Renee said. Still, the company of her friends helped. She managed to smile and swung into a Mozart fantasy that always pleased them. Friends, she knew, were what really mattered in the everyday world. Love had only brought her sorrow long before she came to Sunrise. The love she had now would endure as long as Sam lived—and beyond. It would have to be enough for now. She could hold tight to faith, believe in his faith. In her checkered past, never disclosed to a living person, she had never met a man like Sam, nor one who compared with him in any way, including in the arts of love and quiet communion.

Donkey said, "About time to make the rounds. Maybe tomorrow's mail, Renee, huh?"

"That's right." She stood up, tall and straight, smiled at her friends, and said, "I have a fine brandy upstairs. Join me."

It was good to be with the three of them: the old man, the youth who worked at the bank, and the bride who had been a dance-hall girl and was still a lady. It would do until Sam came home.

The lightning flashed. Sam Jones said, "Moseby, you wouldn't be worth a fiddler's itch out there. You stay and watch for trouble at the house."

"You said there'd be some shootin'," Moseby complained.

"You'll get your fill," Sam told him. "Francisco, you stay, too."

"Them steers are so spooked now, any damn thing can happen," Pit muttered.

"Stubby's out there with the boys. It's you and me, now." Sam turned toward the stairs.

Pit's voice stopped him. "Best not say a word to Mary."

Sam hesitated. "You're right, I reckon." He checked his step toward the stairway, blinked, stared, and blinked again.

The maverick kid stood on the landing. She wore a long skirt and a white blouse. Her neck was tanned by exposure to the sun, but was nonetheless smooth and lovely, as were the big dark eyes she turned on Sam.

"Well, Miss Mac, you're lookin' mighty fine this evenin'," Sam spoke gallantly. Any thoughts of Mary were quickly gone from the curious faces turned to survey the kid. It was just as the women had planned it.

"Better'n I need to," the kid snapped. "I should be out there ridin'."

"Oh, my, my, now." Sam was unable to keep the teasing tone from his voice. "How many herds have you driven?" he asked with meticulous politeness. "How many stampedin' steers you roped lately?"

She bit back her usual tart answer, biting her lip in order to follow Mary's and Matilda's instructions.

"I reckon Matilda can use you here, as much as we boys will be missing your help outside. That is, if you haven't plumb forgotten what it is young ladies are supposed to do."

Sam saw the flush creep into her face, but she answered him evenly. "Mary said you should look out for Stubby, but she didn't say who should look out for you."

Surprised by her easy acquiescence, Sam nodded, his mind occupied with trying to anticipate all the troubles this night would surely hold for the Crooked S and the people for whom he had made himself responsible.

He still heard the taunt and goaded back, "Don't you

worry yourself none over me, missy. It's a wild night for weather, and anything might happen, but I've gotten through the likes before.'' He wished he was as confident as he sounded.

"Well." She paused. "You look out, will ya?"

"Yeah," he drawled, "and you give Matilda a hand. She'll be busy cookin' for those who can get back for food."

"Sure will," she assured him, stepping halfway down the stairs. Dainty slippers and a whisper of black stockings momentarily bemused Sam, but then he turned for the door.

Her voice stopped him, and he turned to see the maverick in her eyes, straining against what she had been told to do. "Duffy's out there." She pointed. "He's aiming to do harm. He's got a damn army to help. I should be lookin' for him."

"I'll be keepin' an eye out," he told her.

"Yes," she said, "but I don't want to miss the chance." Her voice was the kid's again, wild and steady. Her tiny hand clenched into a fist.

"Look, kid, if the cows start runnin', it'll be his herd as well as the Crooked S bunch. It'll be dark as the inside of a boot, and who's to know what from which? Further and more, you can keep an eye out right here. You and Moseby and Francisco, that ain't an army, but it's three good people. Leave Duffy to me."

After a moment, she nodded. "If anybody, it would be you, Sam."

"Well, now, let's not go all headlong," he said. "It's just that he can get in my way as well as anybody's and I'd sure like for that to happen."

She stood only one step above him now, bringing her head just even with his chest. Suddenly her face softened and she threw her arms around him. "I know. I know. From the first damn time, when you pulled them kids off me, I knew. Don't you get hurt, Sam Jones. Please, don't you get hurt.''

He held her awkwardly. "Now, now, kid. We'll talk about you and Duffy and whatever when this night's over. You take care of Mary and keep a gun handy.''

She released him and fled up the stairs. Sam exhaled a deep breath. The maverick kid, a lovely young girl, still sought vengeance on Duffy for reasons unknown; and, he divined, she was a bit too personally interested in one Samuel Hornblow Jones.

He stopped in the kitchen where Pit waited with Francisco and Moseby, who was still making noises about being left out of the action.

Sam and Pit left Moseby grumbling in the kitchen and went to the horses. The storm was lashing them now; it was nearly a gale.

Pit said, "Hell to pay, for sure.''

Matilda burst from the house to intercept them before they could mount.

She shouted into the wind, "Here now, you good-for-nothing men. Don't you ride off and leave me with that sick man in the bunkhouse. That man, he real sick. Talkin' 'bout some captain or t'other'll be on his butt. We need a doctor here.''

"Can't be helped, Matilda,'' Sam shouted.

"Well, I wants him in the house so's I can watch him,'' she insisted, the wind swirling her skirts against her legs.

"Get Moseby and Francisco to help bring him in and keep an eye out as best you can. Those Comanches may take a notion.''

"And just be damn glad you don't have to ride,'' said Pit, as he mounted his horse. "We best get moseyin', Sam.''

Matilda snapped, "I could ride, too, like as not as good as you, old man. You just watch out for yo' ownself.''

As they turned into the storm, Pit said to Sam, "That Matilda's one fine woman. She's taken care of Mary Stone like a mother. But she can't ride worth a damn. Let's get outa here."

Sam sat astride the roan, which was not a cow pony by any means but had responded well in all situations up until now. He said, "It's been a long time since I worked cows in a storm."

"Keep close. I ain't as young as I once was, but I know what's what," Pit said. It was the blackest of nights, and the rain swept one way and then the other. The lightning flashes were welcome in showing the way. "We'll head for the river. Stubby and the boys will be tryin' to cut them off from going into the drink. If we had a dozen more hands, I'd feel a hell of a lot better."

"Seems to me Duffy's got the same problem," Sam allowed. "Exceptin' he's got more men."

"Most of which don't know the land too good." They rode on toward the Pecos. "Trouble is, will they take to shootin' at us?"

"Pickin' targets won't be easy on a night like this," Sam said.

"Uh-huh. 'Ceptin' we care who we hit."

That was true. Such guns as Duffy hired had no love for each other. Sam wondered about Jackson and Magrew, who were partners. They were the most dangerous, of course. He thought somberly of the man he had killed, the man called Max. What had been his connection with the Duffy contingent? How much did his demise mean except that it could be held against him, as murder while escaping from jail? If Keen did not recover, and Duffy told convincing-enough lies, the Rangers would have a lot of questions to ask of Sam Jones.

They pushed on to the river, now higher and swifter and deeper. They followed the bank until they heard the familiar clashing of horns that meant they had reached the herd. It was certain that, even short-handed, Stubby had pulled it together so that it could be more easily patrolled. A convenient slash of lightning identified that worthy sitting his mount directly ahead. Pit called out to identify himself, and the trio came together.

"Figured you'd be along this way," said Stubby. "How was Mary?"

"Perked up. Her and Mac playin' house, like," said Sam. "Moseby and Francisco are standin' by."

"How's the Ranger?"

"Matilda says bad. She was going to have Moseby and Francisco help her get him up to the house."

"We got our hands right full," said Stubby. "They're gettin' restless. Ain't heard nothin' from Duffy's bunch."

"Trouble is, even our druthers ain't no good," said Pit Pickens gloomily. "If the cows go to Duffy's, that'll be hell. River's worse. The road? They could go all the way to town. And they will truly raise hell with the chickens, if they go toward the house."

Stubby answered, "They been through storms before is why they ain't started yet. It'd take somethin' special to get 'em going, I figure."

"Somethin' special is what allus happens," growled the old man. "I'll just take me a look-see." He rode down to the river's edge.

"I sure dragged you into it," Stubby said. "I thought— well, damned if I know just what I did think. You always had more smarts than me. Reckon I figured you'd think of somethin' that'd take Duffy off my back. It was plain, rotten selfish of me, that's what it was."

"Podner, you were worryin' for Mary and the baby," Sam said. "So you sent for me. I'm right proud."

"Hell, I dunno what to say, Sam. I—"

"Talkin' won't do it right now, will it? Which way you

think we ought to ride?'' With stunning speed, the answer came from above.

The thunder was deafening. The lightning was close by. It struck a dead tree leaning over the river and set it afire. Horns rattled, and the bellowing of steers became louder than the falling rain and the roaring river.

As always, the longhorns milled, clashing, looking for a leader. Sam and Stubby yelled, riding, using their ropes, lashing to keep them going in circles, hoping to dispel the cattle's panic with their own actions. They heard the voices of the other Crooked S riders endeavoring to do the same.

It had been many a long year since Sam Jones had played cowboy, but now he was in the role up to his ears. The fire turned the wild cattle away from the river, but which way the stampede would go was still hidden in the cards, he knew. One thing was certain: The rush was on. Once it started, it could not be stopped until time ran down and men conquered frightened beasts.

It was then that lightning flashed again and the curse of St. Elmo's fire manifested itself. He had gone through this once in his youth on the trail, long before he'd learned that it was anything other than malevolent magic, this manifestation of static electricity that took the form of white, glowing circlets attached to the cattle's horns at the very points, rolling wildly in phosphorescent balls. Nothing drove a herd further into panic.

In the reflected glow, he saw Stubby and then heard him cursing as he still tried to keep the herd from milling, riding too close, dangerously near needle-sharp horns. Sam saw one of the other cowboys circling near Stubby. He could not make out which one it was.

He shouted and used his rope, whipping at the running cattle. The rain slapped at his face, blinding him. Then the roan faltered and he knew why, and he was forced to slow down. Junior was a sound animal, but this work demanded a wiry cayuse that could spin on a silver dollar and give change. He perforce pulled up. The steam rose from Junior's hide; his head went down. To try to drive him further was pointless. On a cattle drive, there would be a remuda from which to find another mount. But here, so far from the corral at the ranch, he was helpless.

As he sat, he realized that somewhere beyond his ken, the herd had found a direction. The drumming was louder and steadier as their hoofs beat the ground. He could not ascertain which way they were heading, and that he had to know.

The ghostly light of St. Elmo's fire limned the tall figure of Pit Pickens riding toward him. Sam hallooed. Pit pulled up, squinting into the strange half-darkness.

"That you, Sam?"

"My horse is stove in."

"Figgers. There's worse. They got a leader, old Satan. And he's takin' them back to the house."

"What about Duffy's herd?"

"Comin' the same damn way. Like they can smell it out. I got to get back there and split 'em."

"Duffy's men?"

"They got a Mex and some of his reg'lars. Mex has a few vaqueros, real good riders. You know what that means with all of 'em running toward the house and the buildings?"

"I'm on my way." Sam knew what it meant, all right. Ruination, unless there was some way to split the running cattle. He knew the problem and he knew the danger. There might be time, he thought, to beat the herd there even on weary Junior. He said, "Red horse, I may have to kill you, but we got to make a try."

He followed the dim figure of Pickens. Now the rain had slackened. The storm was moving away northward to devastate. Junior responded to Sam's urging, having regained his wind.

Sam thought of Mary; of the kid, now a young lady; of Keen, the Ranger; of the inexperienced Moseby; and of the one-armed Francisco. He thought of Stubby racing with the herd, worrying about his wife and his home. He wondered what direction Duffy's big herd would take when the vaqueros got it under control.

In his single-minded preoccupation with immediate problems, he never once gave thought to the way Matilda had gathered her charges into the house.

He rode with all possible haste but took appropriate care. There was a climax approaching and he had to be there when it happened. It seemed impossible, but this dreaded night was almost gone.

The Comanches had managed to recapture their horses except for Soledad's, the best of the bunch, and he had complained, Maizie knew, even though she could not hear what he said. She had seen him snatch a halter from one of the braves and wave him into the darkness before he could protest.

She huddled miserably near the fire that Soledad had managed to build by scraping pulpwood from the sticks she had gathered. The overhanging cliff gave only partial shelter.

Soledad had not questioned her about giving Jones the guns and would not do so, she knew.

She watched in the strangeness and confusion of this night as he pointed toward the sound of scattered gunshots and pushed the young brave whose horse he had taken out of the circle of light.

She watched the brave dissolve into the scrub, knowing he would return with another horse, however he obtained it from its proper owner.

Her own horse had remained where she had tethered him before she had brought in the guns to Soledad.

The Indians waited stoically, rain dripping from their faces, eyes fixed on Soledad as he moved back to the fire.

Maizie knew what they thought of her. She knew that it was too late to change anything. She despaired even as she spoke. "Will you ride for Duffy without the guns?"

"The guns are at the Crooked S with Jones," Soledad answered. "We cannot return to my father without horses."

There was a long silence as they waited for the brave to return with another horse. Unnerved by the quiet, Maizie slipped away from the fire as silently as the brave had dissolved into the scrub. She returned quickly, leading her mount. Handing the reins to Soledad, she said bitterly, "Now you wait no more. You have a horse." She turned away, hearing the braves titter among themselves at Soledad holding the reins to the woman's saddled horse.

Flushed in spite of the cold, Soledad whipped her back to face him and silently handed her the reins. Maizie knew that she had twice shamed him that day.

Any Comanche woman would have gladly died before giving Jones the guns. She had been the cause of bad face for Soledad, and she had thought to make it better by proffering the horse. She now knew that they had already considered taking her horse and that Soledad had rejected the choice. At least, she thought, he intended to let her live.

She also knew how long that life would last if the sullen warriors had their way. She hated these men who held Soledad's loyalty in a way that she would never be able to.

Again there was the long silence in which she could hear the rain slackening, see the fire gaining volume.

The sound of gunfire rang out somewhere below them, followed by the eerie chant of the Comanche victory song ending on a triumphant note.

"Now, we have horses for all," Soledad said.

He grimaced, barking a laugh to impress his braves. "You say fight for Duffy. You say fight for Jones. We fight for guns and horses, and we care not whose they are.''

''You will die.'' And she knew as she spoke that they were true words.

''Then I will die a Comanche.''

The young brave strode proudly into the circle of fire-light with his right palm out to signify the success of his mission. As if everyone could not see the cow pony that he led, Maizie thought.

''We have horses for all.'' The brave spoke with a challenging edge, glancing sideways at Maizie's horse.

''Any dead?'' Soledad asked.

''None of our people,'' replied the warrior proudly.

''The gods have turned their face to us,'' Soledad said gravely.

He was not unintelligent, this savage who tore her heart. He would be faithful to his father's teachings, she knew, but she could not resist one last try. ''This is foolishment. You ask for the dead? You will all be dead before this night ends.''

Soledad turned to her, his face a mask of fury. ''You name me fool, woman. Who gave Jones the guns?'' He mounted and turned, signaling the others, and rode, almost without sound, into the confusion of the stormy night.

Maizie's breath rasped in a sob as she called into the darkness, ''Go with God.'' She knew that their days of riding free, the days of the moon raids, were ending.

There was no answer to her cry. Not even the sound of riders in the brush. She stood stiffly, listening, and then broke like a sawdust doll to sink by the fire and finally, truly sob out her shame and loss into the wet dirt.

In the arroyo, Soledad faced a messenger from his father. The man was called Dogface; he was ugly but clever, the son of a minor chief.

Dogface said, "Your father says you are to return at once. You are to join the moon raid."

"My business here is not finished," Soledad replied.

His men groaned, openly deserting him, he knew. His life closed in on him. He sat high in the saddle, facing them, scorning them. "There are guns to be had, horses to be had."

"You have failed. You know it. Our people no longer honor you." Dogface was positive; he had sensed the rebellion in the band, Soledad knew.

He was no longer young and impetuous, and he hesitated. His woman was lost forever, of that he was assured. He had no reason to rebel. He should accept the situation, return to his tribe, and suffer humiliation. He cried, "Damn you. I ride to the sound of my own drums."

One of his own recalcitrant braves fired the shameful shot. It struck him in the heart. He slumped, the startled horse leaped sideways, and Soledad, the Comanche, was thrown into a pile of thorny mesquite. He died there, unsung.

The Comanches were silent for one moment, then they gathered about the new leader.

Sam gave Junior his head. The roan was gaunt but game. Pickens had vanished on his tough cow pony. There was only one thing to do: follow the river road listening to the clatter of horns and the braying of the herd. The cowboys would be working as only they knew how. The real danger would come when the longhorns and men came to the house and outbuildings.

They were all out of Sam's sight, but there was no problem knowing where they were, charging heedlessly behind the leader they had found. The problem lay in whether or not he could get to the ranch ahead of them.

He came at last to the path leading from the river to the ranch house. Junior staggered making the swing but gathered himself gallantly for the last run. The voices of the cowboys were distinct now. "Yeeow! Yippee! Yahoo! Swing, you bastards!"

Then he was in sight of the action. He could see Francisco and Moseby and the damn kid, of course, out in the yard, guns in their hands.

Sam rode around the barn and flung himself off the horse with his rifle ready. The riders—Casey, Dobey, Morgan, and Callahan—came driving in on their hardy ponies. Still the herd came, led by a leathery, old, dun-colored steer.

There was a shot. The panicked leader went down, his horns digging dirt. Pit Pickens rode into the scene. He went directly to the fallen steer and began firing over the heads of the charging herd.

Stubby swung away from the cowboys and into line with Pit. It was suicide, Sam thought, his heart sinking. He leveled his rifle and began firing. Steers fell. For an instant, it seemed the racing herd would run over both Pit and Stubby.

Suddenly everyone was shooting. The cowboys shrilled their cries to the sky. Sam killed another of the middle cows.

The herd split. Whooping, the riders were upon them, chivying them each way so that they missed the buildings. It was a narrow squeak. Pit's horse stumbled. Sam began to run, emptying the chamber of the rifle into the air. Stubby reined around. Sam dropped his gun and dove for the fallen old man. He managed to cover Pit with his body.

Cows and horses thundered, but, true to legend, their feet evaded the fallen men.

In minutes, cattle and cowboys were gone, past the house, racing through the garden, headed for distant places.

Stubby swung down from his exhausted pony. Sam got to his knees and peered anxiously at Pickens. Stubby joined him as Francisco, Moseby, and the kid all came running across the yard, past the corral.

Pit said faintly, "Allus knew you could split 'em, if you tried hard enough."

Sam said, "Best get him into the bunkhouse."

"There's a door off its hinges. I'll get it," Francisco volunteered.

"Lemme alone," Pit said. "In a minute I'll get up and do a jig for you all."

"Not today you won't," Sam told him. "You're a mite busted up, old friend."

"Well, we sure busted the gawdamn stampede, now, didn't we?" He grinned up at them. Blood from the corner of his mouth traced the lines of his face.

They lifted the door gingerly as Pit winced. Before they could move, Matilda burst from the door. "Here now, you damn men, you git him in the house so's I can see to him, along with that Ranger man. Lawd awmighty, it don't seem white folks got a lick of sense. 'Specially men." She fumed and fussed, following and bossing them. "All comes from pridefulness, Pit Pickens," she growled. "Thinkin' you know more and ride better'n anybody. Gittin' yoself broke up like I ain't got enough to do without havin' to tend you."

She artfully steered the carrying committee into the big front room, saying, "Put him down on that settee there," first covering it with a soft blanket that she seemed to produce from nowhere in particular.

Sam grinned to see the kid hanging almost on Matilda's skirts as the cook sashayed into the kitchen to get her bag of remedies, and then returned, crying, "Now, whereat's he hurt? You folks get away now. Lemme see to 'im."

Sam studied the kid, right behind Matilda, and thought she had an unfamiliar green cast. 'Bout time, he thought, glad to see her acting more like a girl.

He pulled Stubby out of the nurses' way. Stubby shook his head, looking like he'd been kicked by a mule.

"What is it, Sam? Could you tell?" His eyes filled with tears.

"Looks like his leg, at least. And he had a hell of a fall. I sure hope that horse didn't step on him."

Matilda glared up at him. "I'll find out. Ain't you people got nothin' better ta do than git in my way? I'll find out what's wrong with him."

Moseby took the good arm of a transfixed Francisco and led him toward the kitchen. Looking back over his shoulder, the cowboy muttered, "Looks like a damn hospital, don't it? Reckon we're all lucky to be alive."

"There's nobody like Pit for doin'," Stubby said. "I purely can't do without him. Mary loves the old goat, too."

The Ranger, Keen, stirred on the pallet Matilda had made for him on the floor. He looked around wildly. "What— Who—?" He shook his head.

"Get that man some water." Matilda gestured to the kid. "Mistah Jones an' Mistah Stubby, git on out of here."

Stubby obeyed, moving trancelike into the kitchen where he stopped, musing on what to do next. His concern for Pit had momentarily overcome his concern over Duffy's next move, which they knew was coming.

Sam noticed that the kid had disappeared again, probably to check on Mary, he thought to himself. From the door, he studied Matilda's ministrations carefully.

She glanced at Sam, reached into her bag, and took out a large pair of sharp shears. "Seems like you got a bit more sense'n some I've seen around here." She frowned at Pit, who watched her silently.

"Seen a lot more'n most," Sam said. "That's some bag of possibles you've got there."

"Possibles?" Matilda snorted. " 'Possibles,' huh? That's mountainy man talk," she said as she cut Pit's clothing to determine the damage. "You're too young for talk like that." She held her mouth pursed as if to gentle her touch. Pit sighed and closed his eyes.

Sam smiled at her derision. "I've met a few mountain men in my time. How's the Ranger coming?"

"He comin' fair. Better than he look."

"How come you doctor so fine?"

"When I was South, I was house slave to a doctor man. Good man, treated me fine. I was young then."

"Runaway?"

She gave him a sharp glance, then smiled and nodded. "There was a young buck. We took off on a night like we just had here."

"What happened to your man?"

"He left me for a light-skin gal." She shrugged and laughed. "Don't make no matter. I like what I got here."

"They're lucky to have you."

"I couldn't save the missus's other babies." Her mouth drooped. "They want this one real bad." She shot a look upstairs, but said no more.

"Third time is lucky." Sam spoke offhandedly, glancing at Keen, who was stirring. Pit lost consciousness. Matilda had cut his shirt away and was working on the waistband of his Levis.

Sam said, "Matilda, there's still a lot of trouble coming tonight."

"Duffy," she said, nodding. "Looks like Pit's stove-in. I don't like that bleedin' at the mouth. Sure hope there ain't no rib stuck in his lung."

"We do need the town doctor, don't we?"

Keeping her attention firmly on Pit, Matilda said softly, "We gonna need him more befo' this night is over, Mistah Jones, ain't we?"

Sam nodded, trying to think of a way to get the help he knew was needed, then shook his head. "Just have to do the best we can, Matilda."

He walked softly through the kitchen and stepped outside, so as not to disturb Matilda anymore.

The silence after all the hubbub was unreal. He took a deep breath of the almost dawn air. He had no awareness of needing sleep; the juices were flowing in a rapid stream. He scanned all points of the compass. There was neither sight nor sound of the forces he knew were arrayed out there.

He had to discuss strategy with Stubby and Moseby. He believed Duffy would make an attack in force sooner or later, and was thankful that Stubby had built in stone. Sam was also thankful that Matilda had made them place their casualties inside. He knew the cowboys would be gone far too long to be of help.

Behind him, Matilda bustled through the kitchen, calling over her shoulder to Sam, "Got to have more blankets." She disappeared into the bunkhouse.

Sam paced, resuming his train of thought. There was Matilda to be thankful for, for sure. There was Moseby, the southern gentleman, with his shooting skills. There was the fact that the Ranger and Pit still lived.

Against these assets he weighed the power of Duffy and the possibility that the Comanches might still attack.

His pacing brought him near the bunkhouse. His heightened senses took him a step closer, and a slight sound sent him into action. He dove for the door. As he slammed through it, he saw Matilda backed into a corner. Looming over was the figure of a man, long knife upraised to strike.

As always, without conscious thought, Sam's Colt jumped into his hand, and his finger pressed the trigger. The man dropped, head-shot.

Matilda turned, lifting an arm holding blankets. In the

other hand, she was firmly grasping a hunting knife snatched from Francisco's bunk.

She looked at the body on the floor and shook her head regretfully. She said, "Mistah Jones, I'm plumb sorry you had to do that. I was jus' about ta tear out his guts."

"Who in tarnation is he?"

"Fielder," she said. "He the man tried to git me afore. Mr. Stone fired him an' he went to Duffy."

"I remember." Sam blew smoke from his gun barrel and inserted a bullet. He came close to bitter laughter at his own expense. Always the hero, he thought, and he need not have killed this one with a chancy head shot. The onus could have been Matilda's.

He took hold of the man's worn-down boot heels and dragged him from the bunkhouse. The wound was in his right temple. There was little blood. He pulled the body into a clump of spindly shrubbery, which partially concealed it. There would be no time for burial today.

Matilda thrust a flask into his hand. "Here, you need this, Mistah Jones." The flask came from her ample pocket. It was good whiskey. "You don't think on that Fielder now, he never was no good." She mused, "What goes 'round, comes 'round. You don't think on him now, you hear."

"I think on 'em, Matilda. All of them."

"I reckon. Take another swig."

After taking a long pull from the flask, Sam said thoughtfully, "That man that left you was the biggest damn fool that ever walked."

"Him? Well, that high yellow woman stabbed him one night in El Paso. Killed him dead. Took his poke an' opened a whorehouse. Like I said to you befo', what goes 'round, comes 'round."

Before Sam could answer, she was gone with a swish of her skirts.

As he saw it now, the Crooked S had himself, Stubby,

Moseby, and one-armed Francisco, who had stood goggle-eyed during the stampede. Them, two women, one about to give birth, and that maverick kid, who didn't yet know who the hell she was.

He opened the kitchen door to be confronted by the kid in her new feminine garb. She stood with surprisingly dainty hands on her hips, confronting him with a steady stare.

He wondered again at the suddenness of this child. "Kid, if you want to tell me about it before the shootin' starts, you better spit it out now."

"Why, you know what I was thinkin' of." Her great eyes opened even wider.

"Nope. Just what I'm thinkin' of. Some of us might not get any older than we are today. Best we should know each other."

She glanced at the sleeping men and said softly, "I wouldn't tell this to nobody else in the world. The minute you grabbed me away from those boys in Bowville, I knew."

Sam waited, knowing that if he spoke she would break for cover again, and he needed to know it all.

"You call me a kid," she continued, still pasted to the wall for courage. "I'm no kid. I'm seventeen years old. My father's name was Maxwell Murgatroyd. My name's Maxine. My father owned a fine spread in Mexico. He was killed and, by God, I know who killed him. It was Duffy." The words tumbled out so fast that Sam could not react before she continued.

"I know, Sam. You understand. . . . I know." Her voice rose as though she did not expect him to believe her, but she went on anyway, sounding more and more like an angry, frightened, little kid. "An old vaquero who worked for my father told me the whole thing. You see, he told me the whole thing, and then he went and died before I could do anything about it." She stopped and took a short, ragged breath. "My mother, she was a weak woman. Duffy courted her and she married him, she *married* him, Sam."

It had taken almost everything she had to get this out. She pressed a small, clenched fist against her mouth to stop the flow of words. She fought back the tears.

"Is that where he got his start with money?" Sam asked.

"That, and murder and robbery. He scared my mom to death. He beat her. Then—then. . ." She chewed her lower lip. "He went after me."

Sam started. "How old were you, for God's sake?"

"Fifteen."

"The son of a— So you ran away."

"First I took some money out of the safe, my pop's safe—my pop's money. Then I took a horse and came over the border. I was raised on a ranch. I could scrounge around. Duffy moved to Bowville and stole Stubby's saloon. I kept track. I knew. . . . What I wanted was to blow him away. I still do, Sam. I've earned that, you know I have." She paused for breath.

Sam nodded. "I see. All that, and you had to play a boy to keep the men off you."

"You're damn well right. I never saw the man . . ." She paused, flushed, and looked away. "Then you came along and I knew about the Stones and the Crooked S, and I just did what seemed best. . . . An' now I'm here and Duffy's got an army out there," she finished miserably, her eyes beseeching Sam to understand, to help.

Sam said gravely, not looking at her, "He's got a lot more to answer for than I reckoned. Maxine? That's a nice name. I got a lady named Renee back in Sunrise who'd really like to meet you."

"I know about her," Maxine flared. "I don't need her. Just you and Mary and Matilda, that's all."

"Everybody needs friends," he answered. "All the friends they can get. Seventeen ain't no kid, you're right about that. And you sure do know a lot. But friends is another matter."

"Well, Duffy's got to be stopped."

"Right again."

"He wants to get hold of me. He wants to kill you and take Stubby's ranch and all. . . ." She choked on the thought.

Sam steered her gingerly by the elbow. "We got to eat somethin'," he said. "We got to eat and calm down and start watchin' and listenin' and prayin' that the cowboys get back. It's going to be sudden. These things always are."

"I'm ready." She did not look ready in Mary's pretty dress. She said, "I knew about your lady in Sunrise."

"You do know a lot about everything."

"I ask. I even read postcards. I know the telegraph operator in Bowville. Did you ever write that letter?"

He ladled out the stew. "Never had a chance."

"Maybe—maybe she'll be really mad at you?" Her voice said, I hope.

"Not likely." Then he realized she was teasing him. "Well, what if she is?" he said.

This time Maxine looked him right in the eye. "I told you, I ain't no kid."

Sam bent and fiddled with the damper of the stove. Few women had ever embarrassed him. This one was just a damn maverick kid. He looked at her and she wasn't a kid, not truly, and he had to grin.

Stubby came quietly down the stairs. He stopped and stared around. His gaze fastened on Sam. He said flatly, "Mary's having the baby, Sam. She's having the baby right now!" Sam couldn't think of anything that would have made Stubby any more scared than he was at that moment.

"May the Good Lord be with her, Stubby," he said.

"Lord bless us all," Stubby said dazedly.

Maxine ran upstairs. Sam and Stubby stood silently for a moment in the misty morning light. Sam shifted his weight from one foot to the other. "Well, that's the way it is. Now I 'spect we better all look alive here." He shook the dozing men awake. "Moseby, you and Francisco go get them rifles out from the bunkhouse. Don't want no stray Comanches grabbing off that cache."

Sam saw Stubby looking at him, pleading to be told what to do, how to act. "That's all right, ol' podner." When I knew I was going to cash in all my chips, you were there, Sam thought. Aloud he said, "Stubby, I don't know anything about your stores. When the boys get those weapons in here, it'd help if you could get out ammunition and see that everybody's armed."

"Me, too," Matilda said from the foot of the stairs. She was drenched with perspiration. Maxine followed her into the kitchen.

Stubby looked to Sam for what to do. Sam shrugged and then spoke. "Reckon Matilda's right, old friend. Mary'll be all right, if we win this one. And nothing's gonna be right if we lose."

Moseby staggered in with a horse blanket full of rifles and a minimum of help from Francisco, and dumped them on the floor with a clatter.

"Now," Sam said. "We all know what has to be done. Let's get to it." The room became a beehive of purposeful action.

"We got plenty of guns and ammunition," Stubby said with some hope.

Before anyone could answer, there was a high, whining shout from outdoors. "Halloo, the house."

"That would be our brave Marshal Simon," Sam said, sliding away from the table. "Get guns, keep your heads down, and watch out at every window."

The voice sounded again. "Stubby Stone, we know you

got Cemetery Jones in there. Him and that Checkers. They're wanted by the law.''

Stubby was at the stairs. ''Should I answer him?''

The kid said, ''He's not in sight. He's pure chicken shit, ain't he?''

''Mind your language, girl.'' Sam kept his voice calm. ''Stubby, wait a minute until you get your gun ready. Get Moseby's ready, too. There's too many of 'em out there to take any chances.''

He silently thought of the absent cowboys and dismissed the idea with a shrug. Cowboys—thirty dollars a month and found, risking their lives, working hard hours—were a proud and select species of the West. Given the chance, he knew they would battle to the end for the boss. Sam had ridden with them, had briefly been one of them. He knew they could not get back in time to be of help with the job at hand.

Stubby interrupted his musings. ''We got guns here now. I'm going up to the window on the landing.''

Matilda overrode him. ''Ain't nobody goin' up those stairs but me unless I'm dead, even if I have to be high gun. Ain't nobody shootin' 'round the missus but me,'' she scolded.

''Whatever.'' Sam shrugged off the tirade. ''Stubby, get yourself a place, then wait a minute. Let him yell.''

''We got a legal posse out here,'' Simon shouted again. ''Give up them two and that'll be it.''

''Like hell,'' Maxine said. ''Duffy wants me.''

Stubby looked at Sam. ''Okay?''

''Let them wait,'' Sam insisted. ''Makes them nervish.''

There was a minute of silence. Then another voice, closer by, yelled, ''Hey, they got Fielder. I just found him, head-shot. Deader'n a doornail.''

A shotgun suddenly roared in the living room. The voice outside gave a yelp and was quickly silent. Matilda ducked in from the front room, grinning. ''Butt shot,'' she crowed. "Bet that one won't weep too long for Fielder. That ought to keep them away from my sick folks for a few more minutes." She broke and reloaded the shotgun as she made for the stairs.

Sam said, "I'd feel a whole lot better if Keen and Pit could do anything. You see anybody, Maxine?"

"Call me Mac," she snapped. "No, they're keepin' out of sight."

"We know they're behind the bunkhouse. We got to know they're in the barn. Beyond that there's not much cover. Is Moseby covering the other side?"

"Yep," said Stubby. "You know what? They're goin' to break all our windows. Mary and me, we set a lot of store by them glass windows."

"A shame," Sam said. Stubby was all right. He knew that giving up Sam wouldn't stop Duffy. He knew what had to happen, and in spite of his fears for Mary, he was keeping a stiff upper lip.

Sam felt bad. Here he had come down to help, and the way it was going, he was giving Duffy a fake legal stand. Even if Keen wasn't out of it, they could kill him and swear the deed was done by Cemetery Jones. Everybody knew Cemetery Jones was a killer.

Simon's voice was now a shriek. "Stubby Stone, you got one minute to deliver that murderer. One minute, then we're comin' in."

"In a pig's eye they will," Sam said. "Just keep your heads down, everybody."

He held the rifle loosely, trying to locate Simon from the sound of his voice. He had to allow for an echo, but he thought the marshal was too close to be hiding behind one of the buildings. He sighted into the trees.

Moseby came hustling into the kitchen. "That fool, Pit, says he's got one arm and he wants a gun."

"Give him one," Sam said. "But make him keep his fool head out of sight. How's the Ranger?"

"I'll watch him and the Ranger." Moseby selected a handgun for Pit and went back to Matilda's patients.

"Time's up." The voice was really hysterical now. The voice was Simon's, but the words, Sam knew, were Duffy's. He poised himself beneath the window, pushing the girl aside. There was a crashing sound as shot shattered the glass where she had stood.

Sam leveled the gun on the window frame. He sprayed lead in an arc, directing it at the spot from which he guessed Simon had called. He hoped Duffy would be nearby but knew it was in vain.

Once more they heard Simon's voice. This time he screamed, "I'm shot! They got me!"

Matilda fired from upstairs. Stubby and the kid joined in, and Moseby did, too, from the big front room. Lots of wild shots, Sam thought, but at least the sound might impress them.

There was silence. No one showed himself outdoors. There would be a palaver about tactics now, Sam knew. They had no notion of rushing a house with that much firepower showing.

They would try to pick off the defenders until they could start a fire. That kind always started fires, if only to blame their misdeeds on the Indians. They had not even had the nerve to let down the bars of the corral to free the horses before this could be resolved either way, with or without the Comanches.

Sam conjectured again about Duffy's tactics. He knew they could start a fire, easily, in the bunkhouse or the barn. Either way it would panic the horses, and the bars could not hold them once they were caught in the fire. The Indians would get the ones without broken legs, for sure.

If only he could get outdoors, he thought. If he could just move around and catch a few of them in his sights, he would give them a reason to be nervous, he swore silently to himself. He had been through it before and he knew what had to be done.

On the other hand, the few in the house could hold out against the larger numbers outdoors as long as there was no concerted rush.

Duffy's people would never make that charge. And the cowboys had to return sooner or later, he thought. But what if they rode in without hearing gunfire?

The tension inside of Sam was unbearable. He opened and closed his left hand making a fist as he moved restlessly but cautiously about the kitchen.

He could not stand the thought of Stubby losing his property, his remuda, maybe even his life to these cowardly bastards who would not even show themselves. And the baby was coming.

He watched through slitted eyes for the first wisp of smoke, his hand still opening and closing spasmodically.

There was desultory firing. All of Stubby's treasured glass was gone. No one inside had been hurt, but there had been no gain either. He kept looking for the wisp of fire, hating the thought.

The shooting outside slackened. Now, Sam thought, now, you bastards! And he was right. It came from the bunkhouse, closest to the house and the safest cover for them. There was dense black smoke; they had used coal oil.

Ah! He exulted silently as a breeze came, sweeping the smoke toward the house. In a flash, he was out the door, pausing only to call, "Cover me!" as he raced for the bunkhouse.

He had only the cartridges in his rifle, but he had picked up an extra revolver and stuffed it into his belt as he went. He heard the anguished, stifled cry of the girl behind him, but nothing mattered now except that he be allowed to act.

He burst through the bunkhouse door. There were two

of them in the room. He was careful, even deliberate, and then there were none.

He hoped the noise of the barrage from the house had covered his shots. He did not even glance at the bodies on the floor. He went for the window.

He could see two men shooting at the house. He cut them down without compunction. The smoke was becoming too heavy. He was beginning to choke. He went for the open window, climbed through, and crouched beneath the eddying smoke cloud. He took a deep breath and hurled himself toward the corral, jumping the fence. The horses were milling, but were calmed as he spoke to them in a reassuring tone. The bunkhouse was doomed, and rage caused nausea to clutch at his throat.

He could hear Duffy's men calling to each other but could not distinguish the words.

He saw one of them crawling toward the corral. He shot the man, and for a moment he paused, on the brink that always thrilled him, the verge of action. The thrill was mixed with the fear of death.

The steady firing from the house had not ceased. There were good people in there, the best. If he knew how many were with Duffy, it would help. As it was, he realized that his only chance was to try for the leader and finish him before his gunmen could prevent it. That, he thought, would be the salvation of the Crooked S, and Cemetery Jones, also.

If he charged blindly and failed . . . Well, he dared not dwell on that.

The smoke came again, heavy, so that he flattened himself on the ground. His composure was severely shaken when a choked voice close by said, "Well, here we are again."

Sam said, "Damn you, Stubby."

Stubby grinned through his smoke-blackened face. "You think I'd let you go it alone, ol' podner?"

Sam could feel his eyes tear. He hoped it was the smoke. "You got Mary and the baby. . . ."

"No good, if Duffy gets us!"

It was true. Sam said, "If I could figure just where Duffy's at, we could try for him."

"They're looking for us at the house. They'll cover."

"Yeah," Sam said, "if they can see us in the smoke."

The smoke billowed, fickle in the wind. It was too chancy by a thousand, but it had to be attempted, Sam thought.

Then he heard Duffy's voice booming. "Jones is outa the house. Find him, me boys. Find him, and it's all over."

"Got him!" Sam hissed. "Yonder in the trees."

"Shall we dance?" asked Stubby.

"He'll have those two fast boys with him, y'know."

"Seen those kind before, ain't we?"

"When the smoke changes."

"I move with you, podner."

Even if it worked, Sam thought, it would depend upon the Ranger regaining his senses to testify. He put down the rifle and took a revolver in each hand. If only he knew how many they had to face . . . The smoke started to lift and it was too late to wonder anymore.

They went over the corral bars together, then separated to make themselves a double target. They started for the sparse trees from which Duffy's voice had emanated.

Too late they realized they had bought trouble beyond their capacity to react. Duffy was there. And, in addition, Jackson, Magrew, and four riflemen were in the group.

There is ritual to such a showdown. Sam shot Magrew with his left hand and Jackson with his right. They never had a chance to draw. Immediately he dropped to his knee and managed a lateral move. Stubby did exactly the same.

Duffy seemed transfixed, his mouth open. Sam and

Stubby took care of two of the riflemen, who were stupefied by the sudden attack and had fired over their heads.

Stubby was laying down a deadly barrage. It was a war, Sam thought, and the odds were still too great.

Suddenly there was a wild cry and a rider came from Duffy's rear. His men turned and were shot down.

Sam said, "I'm damned. It's Maizie."

Duffy suddenly came to life. He threw both hands into the air. "I give up," he whined. For a split second, Sam hesitated. Then from behind him he heard a familiar voice say, "No you don't this time, you murdering bastard." There was the roar of a shotgun. Even as the derringer slipped into Duffy's quickly dropped hand, the blast caught him. It blew him to eternity in the wink of an eye. "I know that old trick of his with the little gun." The girl turned her horse triumphantly toward Sam. "I told you I ain't no kid," Maxine Murgatroyd said. Her face was smudged with smoke and her new finery some the worse for its use this night. She jammed two shells into the shotgun she carried. "Gave him both barrels to make sure."

Stubby, delighted, called, "Where is everybody?"

Those not on the ground, wounded or dead, had disappeared. Maizie sat her horse and said, "I had no other place to go."

Stubby, always the gentleman, said politely, "You're purely welcome here."

"The baby," Maizie said. "I kept thinking of your wife and the baby."

Stubby said, "Oh, my God! Mary."

As one, they turned toward the house. The dead lay where they had fallen. The guilty wounded would wait. There would be a time and place for attention to both. Maizie followed the group back to the house.

They entered the kitchen to a chorus of questions from Pit, Moseby, and Francisco. In the general uproar, which, by this time, even involved Keen, no one noticed as Matilda came quietly down the stairs. She stood quietly, waiting for some attention, and when none came, she said, loudly, "If any of you 'spects to eat here today, you better take this young 'un off my hands, 'cause I do declare, he is a pure handful."

They gathered around a table in Antonio's restaurant across from Duffy's Place, which now bore a repainted sign that read STUBBY'S PLACE; Sam and Moseby and Ranger Keen and Maizie and Stubby and Maxine. Sam had been there too long; he was restless.

The Ranger said, "Yep, right from the governor. Maxine Murgatroyd is sole heir to everything owned by Duffy."

"It's a partnership," the kid insisted, not for the first time. "Stubby was cheated outa the saloon. Even if he wasn't, I couldn't run it anyway and also take care of the ranch. Pit, he's in on it, too. An' I hate Sam Jones for not takin' a share." But she dimpled as she spoke that last.

Sam said, "You might turn it over to Matilda."

Everyone stared. Then the kid spoke. "Damn. Sam's dead right, as usual. Without her we might not even be here."

The Ranger added, "That Harvard doc, he said she could hang out a shingle any time."

Stubby said, "She brought my baby boy into the world, too."

It was a fine baby, Sam thought, although he had scant experience with those small animals. He had left the horse, Junior, as a gift for Sylvester Nathan Stone, Jr. Stubby's carriage waited at the curb to carry him to Pecos and the stage to Sunrise.

Antonio bustled. He was already a figure of importance in the town, which seemed to have come out from under a cloud into bright sunlight. Everything was fine in Bowville, but Sam yearned for Sunrise.

Antonio said, "I got a fine basket of vittles for you, and one of my pies. Is it true Checkers is going to run the saloon? And Maizie, the gals?"

"So they say." That's what they were all palavering about, bandying words back and forth like conspirators, even the Ranger joining in. It was clear that Keen had an eye for the kid, Maxine "Mac" Murgatroyd. Sam found that easy to discern. Stubby wanted only to get back to the ranch and Mary and his son.

It would all work out, Sam thought. Pit would be the same great help in running the ranch when he recovered. Moseby was honest and also clever. Maizie was lucky in that the Comanches had been satisfied with Duffy's strayed horses and had fled the country to attend the moon raid. She had managed a certain quiet dignity, a quiet acceptance of things as they were. She was now Raven Santos, attired in modest raiments, a force in the town. Yes, everything would be all right, for the time being at least.

He said, "Sorry; folks, but if I don't get goin' I won't make the stage at Pecos."

Stubby leaped to his feet. "Gosh, Sam, I sure hate to see you go. Come back real soon, you hear?"

Moseby pressed his hand. Maizie—Raven—gave him her hand, too. The Ranger half saluted him. They all crowded the walk outside the restaurant.

People stopped to stare at the ballyhoo. Sam climbed into the carriage. On the opposite side, Maxine Murgatroyd leaped and picked up the reins. Before he could speak, she had chirrupped to Stubby's team of bays and they were off for Pecos.

She said, "Wanted a few last words with you, Sam."

"You're gettin' to be quite a talker," he observed.

"Well, you're the first man I ever did talk to."

"You learn fast."

"It's about that Renee. Supposin' she's mad at you 'cause you stayed away so long and never did write that letter?"

"Let me worry about that."

"Well, but just supposin'?"

"I don't play supposin' games. You just mind the road and get me to the stage line."

After a while she said in a low voice, "I just wanted you to know I'd be there."

"Now, Mac, you've growed to be a lady and all that, I do admit it, but I'm old enough to be your father. And—"

"And nothin'," she said firmly. She had resumed her masculine garb: tight Levis and a red and white shirt. Her hair had grown so that it resembled a boy's cap—still, she was all girl. "I'm rich now. Men'll be chasin' after me, you think I don't know it? Well, it'll be a hell of a while before I meet another Sam Jones. I know that."

He sighed. "Mac, you're the greatest kid in the world. Nobody could do what you done. I think you're wonderful. Can we let it go at that?"

After a long moment, she said gravely, "I reckon we can."

It ended there. She drove along the peaceful road to the parting she dreaded without further comment.

But as he was about to board the stage, she leaped high into his surprised arms and kissed him fiercely on the mouth. Then she was gone, fleeing, as he had first seen her in Bowville, swift as an antelope.

Sam dropped off the stage unannounced. The boy named Dink was chasing his dog down Main Street. Sam shouldered his duffle bag and walked to the hotel. He went up to his room and had them bring him hot water, then bathed and shaved and changed into fresh clothing.

When he got to El Sol, there was a welcoming committee: Mayor Wagner, the councilmen, Abe Solomon, Mr. and Mrs. Burr, and Marshal Donovan in the van.

Renee played a rousing march. Shaky, the bartender, called, "Drinks are on the house."

Sam went to Renee. "I'm sorry about that letter. Things got a bit too busy."

"It better be a good story," she said. "Should we go upstairs?"

"Where else?"

In her room, she poured brandy. They sat down across the room from each other.

She said, "You'd better tell me."

Sam sipped the brandy. He thought for a moment and then said, "It's kinda weird, but I reckon the way to start is not with Stubby. That got settled. Y'see, there was this maverick kid. . . ."

About the Author

William R. Cox has been writing for more than sixty years, and has seen over seventy-five of his books and more than a thousand short stories into print. He has also written numerous movie and television screenplays, including episodes for *Bonanza* and *The Virginian*. *Cemetery Jones* was the first book in this, his newest series of western novels. Cox lives in California with his wife, Casey.